Sherlock Holmes
and the
Yule-tide Mystery

By the same author

Sherlock Holmes and the Yule-tide Mystery

Val Andrews

**BREESE
BOOKS
LONDON**

First published in 1996 by
Breese Books Ltd
164 Kensington Park Road, London W11 2ER, England

© Breese Books Ltd, 1996

ISBN: 0 947533 11 7

Front cover image courtesy of
Retrograph Archive Limited

Typeset in 11½/14pt Caslon by
Ann Buchan (Typesetters), Middlesex
Printed and bound in Great Britain by
Itchen Printers Ltd, Southampton

CHAPTER ONE

There is a magic in the very name of Christmas and the words are those of Charles Dickens rather than your humble scribe but, looking back over so many years, I have to say that it is more true of the yule-tides of my youth than those that I have more recently experienced. Towards the end of the last century for instance, when Queen Victoria was still on the throne and all seemed right with the world, Christmas was a magical time indeed.

The goose, fattened since Michaelmas, was something to look forward to for the whole family, as was the pudding taken from its steaming cloth and its brandy ignited. After the meal, stupefied with nourishment the family would gather around the great log fire and the old songs would be sung, the old jokes retold for the thousandth time and many a flirtation would lead to the start of yet another generation.

It was in the early 1890s that this festive season neared once again and even a staid medical man such as I could be forgiven for going about his business with a slight feeling of excited anticipation. Of course there would be the inevitable scrooges among the population who would show little interest in the coming festivities and one of these, I knew from experience, would be my friend Mr Sherlock Holmes. At the risk of encountering a reception interspersed with stuff and nonsense, I decided to drop in at the old rooms in

Baker Street to wish him the compliments of the season.

I had seen all too little of Holmes since my marriage, though I continued to keep in touch with him as much as my busy professional life allowed, lest his lone occupation of the rooms at 221b Baker Street should affect that dark side of his character which tended towards the melancholy.

'My dear Watson! It is good to see you and I trust that you will not be too lonely over Christmas whilst Mrs Watson spends it with her family, not to return until well into the new year?'

I started, 'Holmes, how could you, even with your amazing powers of deduction, know about my most intimate family arrangements?'

He was looking well and alert, despite being leaner than ever. He said, 'Oh come, my dear fellow, there is no great mystery here, surely? The first thing that I noticed as you removed your greatcoat was a scrap of tinsel upon your jacket lapel and a pine needle upon its sleeve. So here we have the picture of a man who can justly be accused of having recently been decorating a Christmas tree.'

I was puzzled and said, 'Come, surely that is a normal seasonal activity?'

He agreed. 'Certainly, Watson, but not several days before the event. You and your manservant would by tradition decorate the tree on the very eve of Christmas. Why, I ask myself, would you therefore be decorating yours several days earlier than is usual. I imagine that the answer is that your wife would be otherwise unable to share its delights with you. She will not return before twelfth night, otherwise she would be able to enjoy the sight of your handiwork later. I note also that she has taken the servant girl with her.'

I exploded. 'Now that you could not possibly have deduced.'

He smiled enigmatically and said, 'On the contrary, Watson. Had the girl been still at your home she would have brushed the clues from your jacket.'

Of course it all made perfect sense when thus explained as Holmes's deductions always did. His methods, though, were not laboriously worked out and long use of his mind in such directions had made such deductions second nature to him. Yes, it was the speed of his findings that always amazed his listening beholder.

I decided to put his powers to a further test, asking, 'And the time involved last evening?'

His gimlet eyes softened almost to a twinkle. 'I cannot be exact, I can only say that it was somewhere between five and six of the clock.'

I said, 'An inspirational guess upon your part, admit it Holmes.'

He rounded on me. 'I never guess, I always deduce. You are, as we have established, a creature of habit and I know that you arrive home promptly at five each evening. Usually you start to dress for dinner at six, so if you had decorated the tree after that time the tinsel and pine needle would be upon your dinner jacket and I would not even have seen them.'

There was such an infuriating logic in it all and yet I could only admire the process of his brilliant mind, even after so many prior examples.

I said, 'To think, Holmes, I only dropped in to wish you a Merry Christmas, and you immediately remind me of the great times of our association. Married life has been agreeable enough I'll grant you, yet I often dream of the speckled band writhing its way down the bell rope and that affair that almost ended in a Bohemian scandal.'

He smiled kindly. 'My dear Watson, one cannot have

everything one would wish for in this world. Count your blessings, my dear fellow.' As he said this he glanced wryly at the portrait of Irene Adler.

We sat before a roaring fire, its mantel uncluttered by the trappings of the season, and indeed its everyday trappings would have left little room for such items.

We smoked our pipes and he passed the decanter, saying, 'Watson, I do wish Mrs Watson and you the very best of the festive season. I am not perhaps quite the scrooge that you might imagine me to be. The ghosts of Christmas past, present and yet to come may visit me with equal freedom. I have made mistakes, yet have never wittingly harmed anyone who deserved no ill: to quote Clive of India, "I have shown the state some service".'

I had to agree, but added, 'Do you not find it depressing to be all but alone in not keeping Christmas in the traditional way?'

Holmes quickly returned to his habitual crustiness. 'What I do find depressing is the yearly display of over-indulgence by a minority. The vast majority of the population are poor; the barefoot boy has no stocking to hang up, even assuming his parents had anything to put into it on Christmas Eve, if indeed he has parents at all.'

So I had arrived full of goodwill to all men, and to Sherlock Holmes in particular, yet it all seemed to be a lost cause. I fell into an uncomfortable silence.

A sharp rat-tat at the front door produced a shuffling of Hudson's feet and then voices on the stairs. Holmes glanced at the clock and then at his hunter as if to assure himself that the clock was accurate.

He said, 'This will be Mr James Harding whom I have never met. He has an appointment to see me, is well built, young in relation to ourselves and impetuous by nature.'

He chuckled, 'Oh come, Watson, only an impetuous man would negotiate that heavy old knocker of ours when there is a bell pull. That he is young and strong I deduce from the manner in which he manipulates the knocker and he has not the patience that a few more years would give him. You see his appointment is for noon but it is barely a quarter to that hour.'

It was nice to see Mrs Hudson again, for it had been Billy who had admitted me. She smiled and said, 'Why doctor, how nice to see you. Mr Holmes, there is a Mr James Harding arrived. He is a little early. Will you see him now?'

Holmes nodded. 'Certainly, Mrs Hudson. Show him in if you would be so good . . . oh and Watson, you are more than welcome to stay and hear what Harding's problem is. Quite like old times, eh?'

James Harding proved to be a well-built young man of about twenty-eight, tastefully dressed in town clothes, including a long dark greatcoat with a fur collar which he turned down now that he was out of the cold. He seemed alert, eager but not agitated and enquired of my friend, 'I am addressing Mr Sherlock Holmes?'

Holmes nodded and said, 'Yes, this is my friend and colleague Dr John Watson, before whom you may freely speak.'

Harding nodded to me in friendly fashion saying, 'Doctor, I am glad to meet you also.'

He was soon comfortably seated and gratefully accepted some port from the decanter, though it seemed that he could scarcely wait for such niceties before saying, 'What I am about to present you with might not sound much like a problem. You see, I have been invited by a mere acquaintance to make up a party to spend Christmas with him at his stately home.'

9

Holmes said, 'I agree that it does not sound like a problem. After all, Mr Harding, if you are even slightly in doubt regarding the invitation you have only to politely decline it. Tell me, where did you meet this philanthropist and what manner of a person is he? I take it we are speaking of a man?'

He replied, 'I met him at the theatre, I was there with friends and we got into conversation during the interval in the stalls bar.'

'Did your friends know him?'

'Why no, he was a complete stranger to us all. A Mr Gerald MacMillan, a well-dressed jovial and ruddy-faced man in middle age. He told me of his stately home, an Elizabethan manor near Henfield in Sussex. It is called Shaw Manor, by which I deduce that it was not inherited from his own family.'

Holmes glanced at me and I cleared my throat and said, 'I can only repeat what Holmes has already said. If in doubt why not refuse? You could do so with every refinement of manner.'

Then he said, with a manner of suppressed excitement, 'Yes, Doctor, but I was intrigued, especially when he mentioned that I could bring several friends, two or three or even more. He said that we could stay from Christmas Eve right through to the New Year. Do you not find this prospect interesting?'

I had to agree that I did and Holmes said, 'I too would have been too intrigued to dismiss the invitation without consideration. I can understand to some extent a generous and impulsive man inviting a complete stranger to whom he had taken a liking to his country home for Christmas. What puzzles me is his extended invitation for you to bring several friends completely unknown to him. Come, I am glad that you have brought this intriguing little happening to my attention, for it is after all the festive season that of goodwill to all men, according to Watson. Even a hardened consulting detective can afford to indulge himself in the investigation of something seemingly trivial just for once. You should make up a party, Mr Harding, and take them to Shaw Manor for Christmas. Make sure that they are solid people upon whom you can rely, whatever might happen. I feel positive that nothing untoward will take place, but you can never be too sure. Should the affair turn out to be of a sinister nature be certain that your companions are strong in mind and body.'

Harding's handsome face lit up. He said, 'I was hoping that this would be your advice, sir, for there is something about the whole enterprise that attracts me. The vague possibility of being lured to this manor house for reasons more sinister than eccentric appeals to the adventurer in me. Doctor, you are an old soldier and a veteran of the Afghanistan campaign so I feel sure you will understand my feelings.'

I asked, 'Is my military past such an open book, sir?'

He laughed. 'Well, you are still a fairly young man, yet you have a gammy leg which you make little of. I notice also that your moustache is still trimmed and waxed in a military manner and that the room contains quite a few objects and artefacts that have originated from Afghanistan.'

Holmes clapped his hands. 'Capital, Watson. We have here a man after our own hearts. But why should such a man, with his own antique business in Guildford, unmarried, ambidextrous and a fair shot with a revolver require the assistance of Sherlock Holmes?'

Harding chuckled. 'You have answered your own question, Mr Holmes. For whilst I am observant and alert of mind I have no idea how you could know quite so much about me.'

Holmes held the attention of us, his audience, by fussing with his briar which he evidently favoured that day.

Then he said, 'That particular chalk dust which I have observed upon your shoes is found mainly in the Guildford area. Your knowledge of oriental artefacts rather points to your occupation. Your very frequent handling of a heavy revolver shows its marks equally upon your hands. Therefore, if your time has not been wasted you are an excellent shot, probably with both hands.'

There was a short silence which I broke. 'Holmes, could you spare the time? My wife is away and I had already arranged for a locum long before I realized that she would be going.' I hesitated and played my last card. 'Holmes . . . it *is* Christmas!'

A rather longer silence was broken by Holmes. 'Upon my word, why not? Come, Harding, if you would like to make the arrangements, Doctor Watson and I will be happy to form your small party for Christmas at Shaw Manor.'

Once this tryst had been established Holmes asked the delighted Mr Harding a few more pertinent questions. 'What was MacMillan's manner towards these friends with whom you were in company when he met you?'

'Oh, polite, but not effusive; not as friendly as he was in speaking to myself.'

Holmes nodded thoughtfully. 'I see. And what manner of people are they?'

Harding gave us an honest, open smile. 'They are artisans, a couple of chaps who assist me in the transportation of antiques.'

Holmes would not leave the point. 'MacMillan did not

then suggest that they should be included in the party for Shaw Manor?'

He said, 'He didn't, but he did not of course suggest that they should not be included. As it happens they found him a little standoffish and would not, I feel, have fallen in with any such proposal. He had, after all, made the suggestion that I bring some friends of my own kind, though without implying that the company concerned would not fall into such a category.'

My friend was thoughtful for a moment, then said, 'One last question, Mr Harding, before you begin to feel that you have become a victim of an inquisition. Do you imagine that this Mr MacMillan has extended such invitations elsewhere and, if so, upon what scale do you consider they might be?'

Harding looked a little bit puzzled. 'I had wondered about that too, Mr Holmes, but I have no way of establishing an answer.'

Harding left us, elated that we would join his party for Shaw Manor and promising to be in touch with Holmes concerning the final arrangements.

He did ask Holmes one final question and one which showed how shrewd a mind he had. 'Mr Holmes, when I communicate with MacMillan should I supply him with your real identity and that of Dr Watson, or should I invent fresh characters for you both to play?'

I was a little worried by the prospect of having to impersonate a fictitious person during the whole festive season but need not have worried because Holmes was of the same mind as I. 'No, no, Harding. Watson and I are too well known to make theatrical disguise advised for days at a time. False whiskers and cosmetics applied to the skin would be detected, particularly at the dinner table. I am not saying that such measures have not been taken by myself on occasion, but usually where short and shadowy appearances would only be required. If he objects to us as his guests we will know that something is wrong, I feel, so let us chance scaring-off anything of a sinister nature.'

After Harding had left, Holmes and I discussed the coming Christmas enterprise. Holmes, among his series of scrapbooks, had one upon the subject of stately and historically important residences within the British Isles. 'Shaw Manor, burnt to the ground by Henry the Eighth, rebuilt to something like its former glory by Sir Charles Reynaud in 1660. Villagers in nearby Henfield in Sussex aver that the manor is haunted and the present occupants have great difficulty in recruiting servants. Well, well, Watson. There is nothing more in keeping with Christmas than a jolly good yule-tide ghost. Clanking of chains, and moaning in the bedchamber at night, eh?'

I grunted, 'You know as well as I do that there are no such things as ghosts, Holmes. In fact I know from experience that you are even less likely than I to believe in such nonsense.'

In a rare expression of humour, Holmes said, 'I know and you know that they don't exist, but do the ghosts know it?'

He passed the scrapbook to me as he delved among his collection for another.

I read aloud. 'The present occupant, Gerald MacMillan, is a city financier.'

Holmes studied the second scrapbook which he had taken from the shelf and said, 'MacMillan poses as a financier but is in fact an adventurer and confidence trickster. His most famous deception concerned Christmas hampers. In 1882 he collected weekly payments all over London from hard-working people who were far from wealthy. The idea was that they would pay him or one of his collectors a small sum each week which at the end of the year would amount to several pounds, and in return they would receive a magnificent Christmas hamper containing a goose, plum pudding, mince pies, sweetmeats, wine and many other seasonal delights to a value far in excess of the amount which they had paid. Colourful brochures had made the scheme seem like a godsend to these working-class persons who, by the very nature of their existence, would never be able to save the money in a normal manner towards such a festive feast. Human nature being what it is and circumstances being as they are, any sort of savings box would be robbed by those who had put money into it to pay for other more pressing necessities which might arise. But once having paid the money to MacMillan they could not under any circumstances redeem it save in the shape of the ultimate goal, a Christmas hamper. Even this would not materialize unless all the payments had been received.'

I enquired, 'What is the source of this article, Holmes?'

He laughed. 'During one of my occasional long periods of inactivity I went through all my newspaper clippings and tried to compile composite assessments of many of the frauds and tricksters with which this country has more than a fair allotment. What I have read you is just a paragraph upon the gentleman in question. There are several more pages which mention other extremely unpleasant activities indulged in order to part hard-working persons from money they can ill-afford to lose. Examples include a "Riviera Roulette Syndicate", a chain letter promising wealth if copied and sent to a number of friends and a guaranteed weekly income of five pounds after twenty weekly payments to Mr MacMillan of just five shillings.'

I said, 'Come, whilst I concur that this fellow is a rascal, one has to take into account the greed and stupidity of his so-called victims.'

Holmes said, 'Watson, it is foolish of you to endow the poor and needy with the same degree of good sense as someone as well read and educated as yourself.'

I grunted. He was right as usual.

We spent the afternoon searching the other scrapbooks, particularly those which would seem to hold out any promise of information, such as 'Aristocracy', 'Conflagration', 'Historical Sussex', and so on. I could see little in any of them that might interest us, but Holmes could. Every now and then he marked a place in one of the scrapbooks with an omnibus ticket. There appeared to be a great many of these in the pocket of his robe, seemingly there for the sole purpose of being used as bookmarks. As he usually travelled by hansom cab I could only wonder where they all came from.

As if reading my mind he said, 'You know, Watson, there are actually people who have little better to do than collect these tickets. I performed a service for just such a person recently and he was so grateful that he insisted on giving me all his duplicates. I am often the recipient of unwanted gifts in this way. I have learned through long and painful experience that it is less tiresome to accept than to refuse such delights. Usually I throw away such gifts as soon as the donor is safely out of sight, but I could visualize a use for these, as you have seen.'

I felt a pang of sorrow for the generous fellow who had bestowed what must have seemed like treasure upon his benefactor.

I asked, 'What, pray, was the service that you performed for this collector of horse bus tickets?'

He smiled. 'I managed to deduce which of his friendly rival collectors had stolen his rare and to him almost priceless Chalk Farm to Camberwell Green ticket which had been erroneously printed upon light blue ticket stock.'

There are times when I rather wish I had never asked Holmes certain questions. You see, however mundane the subject, there is just enough intrigue in the answer to force one to press Holmes for even more detail. 'How did you discover the culprit?'

He sounded elated. 'Ah well, I not only did that, but I managed to get the thief to return the ticket to its rightful owner. I have an acquaintance, Groggy Hamburg, who resides in the East End and is an expert forger, or rather was before he became a completely reformed character. But he still has a small hand-press upon which he used to produce extremely convincing bank notes. I showed him a normal ticket, almost the same as the collectable one except for the colour of the card stock. I also showed him a blue ticket from another route which I was certain would be a good colour match. As a favour he printed for me a whole lot of tickets entitling one to travel from Chalk Farm to Camberwell Green. There was a conference of the kind where all these collectors gather and I gave my client a dozen of the forged tickets to take to the event with the instructions to show them widely *en masse* but to part with none of them. The result was as I had hoped it would be; the thief had been one of those who saw the tickets and returned the stolen item by post in an anonymous manner. I was then careful to see that all the forgeries were destroyed once their purpose had been served.'

I was amazed at the furore that could have been caused by a mere omnibus ticket. I enquired, 'Did you manage to track down the culprit by using your methods in a study of the envelope in which it was sent?'

He shrugged. 'Doubtless I could have, Watson, but my

client was satisfied with the return of his prize and did not wish any bad public shadow to be cast upon his great interest or its devotees.'

I would learn later that Holmes, although having destroyed all the forgeries, had salted all his coat pockets with the valuable duplicates.

He all but read my mind, not for the first time that day. 'You are right, Watson. The world is full of eccentrics and seemingly pointless activities. But these pursuits and those who follow them in many ways enrich our world.'

I returned to my house in order to pack a suitcase and a Gladstone, arriving back at 221b that same evening where I discussed our forthcoming excursion with Sherlock Holmes.

He said, 'I am not anticipating anything too sinister, Watson, but I admit to curiosity and the festive season has brought me inactivity, which is my enemy as you know.'

Instinctively I glanced up at the cocaine bottle on its shelf, relieved to notice that it still carried a thin film of dust.

Noticing my glance, despite its innocent nature, he said, 'Upon my word, Watson, you are like some mother hen! I do not feel in need of induced excitement at the present time. Now let us discuss the matter in hand. On the surface we have a seeming jolly and generous man, namely one Gerald MacMillan, inviting an almost complete stranger to his stately home, Shaw Manor, for Christmas, further to bring several friends. But below that surface, ah well, there is a darkness, for we have discovered that MacMillan is a known confidence man, possibly in residence at a stately home that is well beyond his means. Certainly he has not inherited the property so he must have purchased or rented it. He has a game, Watson, but what is it?'

I said thoughtfully, 'Could he be trying to recruit some suitable crowd to whom he might sell stocks or bonds?'

He puffed at a short clay and said, 'You use the word crowd, yet we cannot be sure that he will have recruited other than ourselves and Mr Harding at this point in time. However, I will grant that there may be others and we know not their numbers. But I do not believe that there will be stocks and bonds on offer. If this were to be the case I think we would have been more carefully chosen. He could only surmise that Harding would bring upright and respectable persons.'

I thought in more devious ways, his use of the word respectable having struck a chord in my memory. 'Perhaps an adventuress in a guest's bedroom, with blackmail involved concerning possible scandal?'

He chuckled. 'The badger game eh, Watson? Such an enterprise would scarcely need a stately home. All you need to exploit it is a rented room in Pimlico or Bloomsbury and a painted lady. I think not, but I hope you are not disappointed, my dear fellow.'

I grunted. 'Upon my word, Holmes, has your opinion of me so deteriorated in recent months?'

He laughed. 'No, Watson, only concerning your sense of humour.'

At this point, Holmes went into a brown study from which he would not emerge for perhaps an hour.

Then he spoke. 'My own feeling is, Watson, that some kind of deception is indeed involved but of a fairly minor nature; the conception of a trickster down on his luck and desperate to capitalize his enterprises. At this stage I will not disclose my thoughts further, even to you, for these are mere theory and I never openly theorize.'

I felt at that point that retirement for the night would be my wisest course, leaving my friend to his scrapbooks, theories and, aye, his omnibus tickets too.

CHAPTER TWO

We took a hansom to Victoria Station where we met James Harding, and the three of us installed our persons and our light luggage in a first-class smoker. Harding had taken the trouble to journey up from Guildford rather than make his way directly to Henfield that we might have the opportunity to discuss our Christmas excursion and its possibilities.

Holmes filled a calabash, a task which lasted until we were already past Croydon, and did not attempt to strike his vesta in order to light it until we had sight of the woods at Crawley. As he puffed, the acrid blue smoke was soon to make the carriage rather like a smaller version of one of the rooms at Baker Street (at least as far as the atmosphere was concerned).

His mood became expansive. 'Come, gentlemen, it may well be that we are merely on our way to participate in a really splendid holiday, however much of a rascal our host may have been in the past.'

Harding was intrigued by these words. 'You have established, then, that friend MacMillan is a scoundrel?'

Holmes nodded. 'He is evidently known to the police for various frauds, petty and otherwise, but I suppose we must not judge him until he shows us some sign of harm.'

His eyes twinkled as he continued, 'After all, it is entirely possible for a confidence man to turn over a new leaf; it does not often happen but we must consider the possibility, however remote. I will be more than interested to see how large a party he has recruited and if all of them have been invited in the same manner as ourselves. Have you had any further thoughts upon the matter yourself, Mr Harding?'

The young man who was responsible for our expedition knitted his brows thoughtfully. 'I have thought a great deal during the time since we discarded that sale of bonds theory. You were right, of course, Mr Holmes. The company would need to be more carefully chosen for such an enterprise. But I did toy with another thought. What if MacMillan were thinking to open his home to paying guests and on New Year's Day we should each be presented with a bill for our stay at Shaw Manor?'

At first thought, I considered such an idea to be absurd. I said, 'Come, Harding. Who on earth would pay such an account when presented with it, after having accepted an invitation which had not included any hint of commerce?'

He said, 'Prosperous persons who had enjoyed their stay and wished to avoid any hint of unpleasantness for the sake of those with whom they had conjoined in the whole enterprise.'

I began to see a thread of possibility in the suggestion, adding, 'Or perhaps he could try to make his guests responsible for his bills for food with local tradesmen?'

Holmes spoke at last. 'Now, Watson, Harding's theory is unlikely, but yours is impossible. I have a considerable knowledge of the law of the land and can assure you that such an additional flight of fancy is out of the question. But yes, Harding, I can see some thread of possibility in your belief that the guests might pay some sort of charge from sheer embarrassment, but it is only one step up from Watson's Badger game theory. What could he raise from such a deception, a few guineas perhaps? He could not enforce such a charge. No, we must think again.'

Yes, and think again we did with Harding and I producing theory after theory each more unlikely than the last, though I was quite proud of one of my own ideas. 'Perhaps there will be illicit gambling with thousands of pounds changing hands at the turn of a card.'

Holmes dismissed this by saying, 'One would have to pick one's victims for such a den of iniquity more selectively to make it profitable.'

But Harding rather liked my theory, 'How about small stakes being involved and blackmail with the threat of public disgrace?'

Holmes laughed. 'With MacMillan himself being arrested for running an illicit casino? I think however mutton-headed the guests they would realize the weakness of such a threat.'

At this point we were nearing our destination and we both looked to Holmes to make a better suggestion. He lowered the window, and although we did not welcome the December chill we appreciated that he had the courtesy to knock the dottle from his pipe out into the open air rather than inside the carriage.

He pulled the leather strap to raise the window again. 'Mr Harding, Watson will tell you that I do not theorize but I welcome your suggestions and have given them the thoughtful consideration that they deserve.' The twinkle returned to his eyes as he spoke these words.

Then suddenly there we were at Henfield, with a bustle of activity hardly to be expected at such a tiny rural station.

As a porter helped with the lifting of our larger luggage from the guard's van, I asked him, 'Is it usually this busy at your station, porter?'

He was an elderly ruddy-faced man with a strong Sussex drawl. He said, 'No, sir, but 'tis near to yule-tide and there is a market at Small Dole today.'

I saw farmers and their wives descending with full baskets, obviously with trading in mind, and others who were peering into the same baskets perhaps hoping to save themselves a further journey to the market and gaining Christmas bargains.

I enquired, 'Is it a long way to Small Dole?'

He answered, 'Why bless you, no, sir. 'Taint more 'un a coupla moiles.'

I gave the fellow a shilling and as he touched his cap and smiled his honest open countryman's smile I turned to my companions and asked them, 'Did you hear what he called this Christmas season?'

Holmes nodded. 'Yule-tide, a wonderful word which probably goes back to the old religion, meaning the winter feasting, before the word Christmas came into use. Notice how many of these rustics have branches of *viscum album* in among the other articles in their baskets. Today we call it mistletoe. These people know not why they gather and use it in decoration at Christmas . . . it belongs more to yuletide than to Christmas.'

As we stood on the platform of the tiny station and watched the South Coast-bound train rattle its way towards the sea I wondered rather just how we and our baggage might be conveyed to Shaw Manor. I had been in favour of communication to ensure some sort of an *equipage* being present to meet us, but Holmes had preferred that we sneak up on our destination like some thief in the night or, rather, in the day. I had to see the wisdom of the possibility of catching our suspect unawares.

As the rustics made their way down the lane towards

Small Dole we looked around for some sort of transport. Then it was that I espied an elderly vehicle which might once have been designated as a brougham and its means of propulsion once thought of as a horse.

A downtrodden-looking young man in well-worn tweeds drove the vehicle nearer to us in what I at first thought of as a providential manner.

But then he spoke. 'Transportation for Mr Sherlock Holmes?'

I realized then that Holmes had wired ahead for this cart, which is all that one could call the mouldering vehicle. The seemingly hard-done-by fellow piled our bags and boxes onto the back and then opened a door that we might make the perilous ascent by means of a rickety step. Harding was amused by it all and Holmes, as ever, took the state of our transport quite in his stride and without comment. I alone seemed a little put off by the ancient carriage with its broken wheel-spring and the equine creature which should have been taken to the knacker's yard many years earlier.

I said to the young man as he shook the reins and clicked with his mouth, 'I have less confidence than you of our getting safely to Shaw Manor in this . . . this tinker's cart than you seem to have, my good man.'

I realized that I had been less than polite as soon as the words had been uttered. He rounded on me and the down-trodden side of his character seemed to have been replaced by a little returning pride. 'Don't my good man me, squire. I realize that this brougham has seen better days and Darkie here too, but I charge only a small amount and there is no other vehicle available in this district. You might need to travel as far as Hassocks or Hurstpierpoint to hire better. I came here having suffered financial reverses, with only a few pounds in my pocket. I bought this vehicle for next to nothing and, discovering that the horse was about to be destroyed, I rescued it from being made into hounds' meat. He was broken-winded and had been ill-used so I reckoned that like myself he deserved better from life.'

His statement was so open and honest that it drew from me an apology.

I asked, 'Might I know your name, sir?'

He replied, 'Fox, Arthur Fox.'

I said, 'Well, Mr Fox. I apologize unreservedly for my more than thoughtless remark. Please forgive me.'

He grunted some sort of acceptance, then said, 'Your remark was mild enough when compared with those of the other visitors to the Manor.'

Holmes's ears pricked up at this; he had taken no part in the conversation regarding my rudeness or Fox's problems but now he was interested. 'You drove the other visitors to the Manor, then? What manner of people were they?'

The unbowed Mr Fox replied, 'Why, they were much as yourselves regarding station in life, but most of them were rather more superfluous . . . you know, men and women of some sort of means but little intellect, especially the women.'

A silence followed and we were able to take in something of the countryside through which we were passing. I could see that it was fine sporting country with woods from which rose game birds. There were several large ponds which looked as if they would be inhabited by large and canny carp. Then, after perhaps some eight or ten minutes, we came within sight of a large Tudor mansion.

The driver helped us down with our boxes and bags at the entrance to the drive, despite my entreaty that he take us to the building itself which stood well back from the entrance gate.

He said, 'As I told the others, this is as near as I go to

Shaw Manor or Mr Gerald MacMillan for reasons quite private. I'm sorry gentlemen, but of course if there is anything else that I can do for you during your stay that does not bring me in contact with him you will find me most of the time near the railway station.'

He touched his hat as Holmes dropped some silver into his hand and then slowly turned the horse and drove back the way we had come.

As soon as Fox was out of earshot Harding asked Holmes, 'What do you make of all that?'

Holmes said, 'A man who has lost his proper station in life and gained one of the railway variety. His words — nay the very manner in which they were spoken — told the story of a man who has suffered reverses of fortune. His clothing is worn but expensive. His animosity towards our host may provide some clue concerning our own little enigma.'

As we made to carry our bags up the drive in the direction of the large double-fronted entrance doors they were thrown open and an elderly retainer wearing an apron emerged and walked swiftly if jerkily in our direction. At the same time a number of baying dogs appeared from seemingly several directions and were collared and removed by various gardeners and stable-boys.

Then he, whom I judged to be our host, was framed in the doorway, Harding identifying him as we followed the old retainer who was struggling with our luggage.

'Gentlemen, how delightful to see you. I apologize for that bumpkin with the seedy brougham, but he appears to bear me some sort of grudge. These yokels have strange manners. It could just be that my last gratuity to him was not, in his opinion, up to scratch, what? I would have collected you myself in my dogcart had you notified me of your time of arrival. Harding, pray introduce me to your colleagues, who are as welcome as you to my humble abode!'

Gerald MacMillan was indeed as Harding had described him: jovial, ruddy-faced and middle aged. He was also tall, well built and had a luxuriant head of grey hair. He was dressed as one would expect a country squire in his own house to be. Frock coat, striped trousers and black vest with a watch fob rather than the more usual chain.

Harding introduced us. 'Allow me to introduce Mr Sherlock Holmes and his friend and colleague, Dr John Watson.'

MacMillan all but started at the mention of Holmes's name but checked his reaction in good time. 'Why, Mr Holmes, Doctor, the world's greatest detective and his Boswell are more than welcome to my humble home.'

I noticed that this was the second time within a couple of minutes that he had used the word humble, and yet there was nothing of Uriah Heep in the way he pronounced it. He made an expansive gesture and we entered the house, leaving a small group of seedy-looking retainers helping the old man with our baggage.

A butler took our hats, coats and canes and we were ushered into an immense living-room where some half a dozen people were gathered before a roaring log fire.

We were in turn introduced to Professor and Mrs Glastonbury, Mr and Mrs Coldharbour, Mr Bowser and Miss Finch. The last two named were evidently not together. The Glastonburys were jovial and well fed, the Coldharbours appeared to be just the opposite being both slight, serious but polite. Mr Bowser was an intense-looking young man with gold pince-nez and Miss Finch was, as her name seemed to suggest, rather bird-like in appearance. I placed her age at about five and forty.

All of them were impressed when Holmes and I were introduced, but Harding got a cooler reception which seemed not to worry him in the slightest. Although we were offered immediate refreshment we decided to retire to our rooms to unpack and wash.

The rooms were splendid, with leaded windows looking out onto picturesque if slightly unkempt grounds. Once unpacked and washed I looked in on Holmes and found him still busy at the wash-basin with soap and towel.

Finally he said, 'Well, Watson, what do you make of Shaw Manor so far?'

I replied, 'It's a magnificent house, even if somewhat run down. I notice that the servants are not exactly out of the top drawer but I feel sure that we will enjoy our stay here. What do you make of the other guests, Holmes?'

He replied, 'They are very much as I expected them to be. The Glastonburys may be friends of Mr Bowser, whilst the Coldharbours were probably recruited by Miss Finch. I noticed that she looked at them and studied their reactions to everything. When they smiled at us she did the same, though a fraction in time later. None of them were alarmed by my reputation, Watson, save our host, though his quick recovery all but covered his surprise.'

Holmes dried his hands thoughtfully and then, having allowed me to help him into his jacket, said, 'Let us collect friend Harding so that we may repair to the living room.'

We were ushered to a low tea-table where we were offered and indifferently serviced with some bland cake and steaming hot coffee, the latter more than welcome. We observed the magnificent decorations with fronds of ivy and bunches of holly interspersed with paper-chains and an enormous Christmas tree decorated with tiny candles and expensive-looking favours. From the fir branches there also hung bonbons which, I did not doubt, contained expensive sweetmeats and tiny presents.

The other guests were a little cool towards us with a deference rather typical of such a gathering.

However, eventually Miss Finch made her way over to us and we both rose as she simpered, 'May I join you?' as if being extremely daring.

As we again seated ourselves I started to make conversation, having no great faith in waiting for Holmes to do this.

I asked, 'My dear Miss Finch, are you an old friend of our host?'

Very finch-like she twittered, 'I met him quite recently at a charity-raising affair, "Rainment for the Noble Savage". These poor people, Zulus for example, have to walk and run enormous distances bare-footed, whilst their womenfolk have to go about their daily tasks, fetching water from wells and cooking casava whilst quite inadequately clad, and dear Mr MacMillan is trying to raise funds so that they can have boots and dresses.'

Holmes and I exchanged a glance and I could tell that we were of one mind as to how many pairs of boots and unsuitable dresses the Zulus would receive once MacMillan had collected the donations.

This was borne out by her next remark. 'He is the treasurer, you know. Well, as I was saying, he invited me to this delightful gathering. Of course I was at first forced to decline the invitation, but when he asked me to bring a couple of my closest friends I could not very well refuse it, could I? The Coldharbours are not mere chaperones, Doctor, but dear friends of long standing. By the way, I know it is wicked of me to worry you thus at the festive season, Dr Watson, but I wonder if I might ask your advice concerning . . .'

She tailed off, a little embarrassed, to ask my advice concerning, I imagined, some trivial complaint.

Holmes, realizing my predicament, happily came to my rescue. 'My dear lady, I do trust that your locket has not been lost but rather just mislaid?'

Her eyes widened. 'Mr Holmes, how could you know that I have mislaid my locket?' I confess that his words did rather startle me too.

Sherlock Holmes was in his element. 'First, Miss Finch, may I express the hope that your long engagement was not culminated by bereavement?'

As if in a dream she replied, 'Arthur, my dear fiancé of fourteen years, died about six months ago from consumption. But how, how can you know these things about a perfect stranger, sir?'

He spoke gently and kindly. 'There is a mark upon your engagement ring finger which must have taken some years to form. The ring has been removed and after such a long period the most likely reason for this would be the death of your fiancé. The fact that you do not any longer wear the ring suggests to me that you had it inserted into a locket, which you would doubtless wear at all times. As you are not wearing such a treasured object I can only assume that it is missing.'

There were tears in her eyes and her lip trembled as she implored, 'I suppose you could not also tell me what has happened to my cherished locket?'

Holmes looked impassive. 'When last can you remember wearing or handling your locket, Miss Finch?'

She said, 'Why, it was on Monday evening.'

He asked, 'You live quite alone?'

'Yes . . .'

'Have you had any recent visitors or tradesmen in your home?'

'Why no, none at all.'

Holmes considered. 'It is unlikely then that it was stolen. You have probably merely mislaid the item. Can you remember the circumstances of its removal on Monday night?'

She nodded thoughtfully. 'Why yes, I removed it, along with my bracelets and other things just before taking a bath.'

She lowered her eyelids at this mention of ablutions. She continued, 'I put these things onto a small shelf in my bathroom as is usual at such times . . .'

Holmes interrupted, 'But I notice that you are not wearing your bracelet or any other form of adornment.'

She said, 'Why no, I decided not to bring them, just the locket . . .' She started, 'Mr Holmes, I do believe you have found my locket!'

She delved into her vanity bag and, with an air of triumph, produced a neat gold locket on a thin chain. 'I put it into my vanity bag because I meant to bring it with me, but not the other things because I intended to leave them behind . . . I . . . I forgot that I had done that.'

She simpered and twittered as she departed to tell the Coldharbours about the rediscovery of her locket. When she was out of earshot, Holmes said softly, 'Bird named and bird brained, my dear Watson!'

At the dinner-table our host demonstrated a jollity and benevolence to beguile all but his most sceptical beholder. He charmed Miss Finch, the Coldharbours and the Glastonburys, whilst Mr Bowser was more quietly appreciative.

Holmes and I maintained what I hoped would seem like a quiet geniality. Needless to say Holmes's reputation was not neglected. He dug me in the ribs with his elbow and I took his hint, telling a version of one of his most famous cases. But the audience wanted more and demanded entertainment from Holmes himself.

MacMillan, sensing that there was about to be a lull in the conversation, said, 'Come, Mr Holmes, I assure you that you are not expected to sing for your supper, what? Though I trust you are enjoying yours. I hooked the trout myself only last evening.'

Holmes studied the whole fish which lay upon his plate. It had, of course, been gutted but was complete in all other respects.

The detective spoke drily, saying, 'Mr MacMillan, it may be impolite to question one's host, but I feel forced to remark that the trout upon my plate was trawled rather than hooked, in salt water rather than in the trout stream which I have observed from my bedroom window. The taste of sea trout is unmistakable, and the mouth of this specimen has not been tortured by a hook. The fish was taken more than twenty-four hours ago . . .' He turned to me. 'As an angler, Watson, you will agree that there is a subtle change in the eye of a freshly caught fish after a day.'

I was a little unhappy about Holmes's questioning of MacMillan's honesty of statement. Were we not supposed to be observing quietly rather than expressing any suspicion? I could tell at a glance that Harding and I were of one mind on this point. At the first opportunity I tackled Holmes on this issue.

He said, 'At first I was determined to lie low but I changed my mind when I met our host. He is of course a consummate actor, but behind that benign façade there is an arrogance that would make him chance his arm. Come, Watson, the man enjoys a challenge, but could well be forced into a mistake that would be to our advantage.'

The evening was spent pleasantly enough. Holmes played

chess with Mr Glastonbury whilst Bowser and Coldharbour watched entranced. This meant that I had to try and entertain the ladies with a game of consequences until, at about nine of the clock, MacMillan suggested that we might like a little theatrical entertainment.

Of course, we were all intrigued and were ushered into the drawing-room where a curtained alcove provided a splendid stage. A pianist and a man and his wife who pleasingly sang duets were produced from nowhere and they were followed by a Professor Hercat who entertained us with delightful conjuring tricks and for an encore threw his voice: out of the windows, under the floor and finally into a small wooden lay figure with a realistically moving mouth.

The ventriloquist and his puppet held a spirited conversation concerning 'George Washington who could not tell a lie'; the puppet repeated the story but got all the essential points wrong with extremely hilarious results. Then, as the *pièce de résistence*, MacMillan brought forth from behind a screen a box-like contraption which he referred to as Mr Edison's invention.

The machine is known today as a gramophone but was not so well known during the period of which I speak. At that time it emitted sound through a large attached trumpet when a needle attached to an arm was applied to a moving cylinder. We were treated to a surprisingly shrill rendition of *After the Ball* in a grating soprano. It was a most interesting demonstration of one of the marvels of science. I confess it was my first experience of it. Holmes, who appeared to have been pained by the singers and the conjurer, had shown great interest in the machine.

Some time later we sat around the fire taking a nightcap and enjoying the dying embers of the huge log fire. It still threw out a heat to keep the bitter December night in its place . . . outside the Manor.

Our genial host raised his spirit glass to us and said, 'Dear friends, I hope you have enjoyed your first day at Shaw Manor.' There followed a babble of delighted comments, ranging from most pleasing to really delightful.

Holmes said, 'Mr MacMillan, I really do congratulate you. The dinner was splendid and the entertainment was obviously to the popular delight. As for myself, I was more than intrigued by your demonstration of Edison's remarkable voice-reproduction machine. The icing on the cake, shall we say?'

MacMillan said, 'No extra charge, my dear chap!'

Everybody laughed and the obvious humour of his remark smacked one of our earliest theories squarely on the head.

When all save Holmes, Harding, MacMillan and myself had retired, I took something of a risk in enquiring of MacMillan, 'You have no members of your own family coming to spend Christmas with you, sir?'

Holmes glared at me, Harding looked a little worried, but MacMillan did not falter in his instant reply. 'A very sensible question, Doctor; why does a man who inhabits a huge family manor not fill it with members of his own kin at yule-tide? Well, the answer is that I am pretty well the last of my line and unmarried at that. Save for the odd cousin and an aunt or two I have no immediate family. The ancestral name is Reynaud but I call myself MacMillan for commercial purposes . . . wouldn't do to have a Reynaud in trade, what?'

I said, 'Forgive me, sir. It was not my intention to pry into your affairs.'

He said, 'Not at all. I feel sure that all three of you and

my other guests are puzzled by my curious way of recruiting Christmas company. The answer is that a man of my wealth and position can so easily make friends with the wrong sort of people. The method I chose has produced a small group of obviously honest and decent people with no hint of a social climber in sight!'

There was a lull in the conversation and MacMillan yawned theatrically, saying, 'I don't know about you, gentlemen, but I feel inclined to throw myself into the arms of Morpheus. After all,' he glanced at the mantel clock as if to confirm a suspicion, 'it is already Christmas Eve, or rather its early morning.'

He lit the way for us up the huge staircase where his oil lamp cast an eerie, almost life-giving effect, to the row of portraits which lined the staircase wall. The long-dead faces looked down at us, their faces dancing strangely in the moving light.

MacMillan said, 'I am considering taking advantage of another of Edison's patents . . . light generated from electricity. If certain of my business plans come to fruition I might be able to afford running a wire from Brighton or Lewes.'

As he said this, the light fell upon the paint and varnish that depicted a namesake at least from the Christian variety: 'Gerald Reynaud. 1756 to 1821'.

Christmas Eve dawned bright, with a change in the weather from stormy to a crisp cold period of winter sunshine. Cold it was, but fine, and Holmes and I, having risen early, decided upon a brisk walk before breakfast. Of course, our conversation inevitably returned to that which we had held with MacMillan some eight hours before.

Holmes said, 'Really, Watson, I thought you rather chanced our situation and enterprise with some of your questions.

However, I believe that no damage has been done, for he furnished answers with a facility which did not suggest undue suspicion. The questions were natural enough and might well have been asked innocently by any of our fellow guests. So we have learned a little from his answers, although he has not been as completely open as you might suppose. At least, let us say that he has left out some information concerning his occupation of the Manor. By inference he would have led us to believe that as an heir he has long been in residence. I believe this not to be so, partly through the dossier upon his activities of the last ten years that we have assembled. Also there are the servants. They are a surly crowd, are they not?'

I had noticed this too and said, 'I deduce from this that he has been away from the Manor for a long time and had left it empty, except perhaps for a caretaker. On his recent return he has hired staff not perhaps of the most experienced variety.'

Holmes shook his head. 'On the contrary, Watson. I have noticed that they work about the Manor as if from very long habit; they never falter or appear to be unable to find anything. You are right when you call them surly, but inexperienced they are not. Rather they strike me as a group of people who know that they can behave casually without fear of dismissal.'

I gasped, 'You mean they have some hold on MacMillan?'

He said, 'Not quite that perhaps, Watson, but something almost bordering on it. We can only continue to study the situation and time will supply the answer.'

At this point I could well give the reader some idea of the Manor grounds and their surroundings. The house itself was surrounded by some ten yards of planned though ill-kempt garden, with lawns, shrubs and paving on all sides. Beyond were woodlands, copses and clumps of trees, some of which made it impossible to tell what lay beyond without further exploration. This did not of course apply to the front of the house which had the long drive from the lane. We decided to take to this country road and, knowing well what lay between the entrance to the drive and the railway station, we decided to take the lane in the opposite direction.

After walking some forty yards, past some cattle pasture on our right and the continuation of the Manor grounds to our left, we came upon a small house which in its Tudor style rather matched that of Shaw Manor. The house had a small but extremely well-kept garden surrounding it with rose bushes and an ornamental pond. An elderly lady of charming appearance was watering a flower bed as she looked up to greet us with a smile. We of course raised our hats and smiled politely.

We passed on and Holmes remarked on the little Tudor cottage. 'Watson, I believe that the small house we have passed once served as a keeper's lodge. Possibly in times past the drive wound so that the little building would have been at its entrance. Obviously it is still within Shaw Manor's boundaries. But the lady in the garden is no mere pensioner or servant. Did you notice her hands, Watson? They have never needed to perform tasks beyond those which they presently undertake. Her hair obviously occupies a great deal of her time and it has been ever thus, for one can see from the length of her plaits that it has never been cut.'

I confess I found this information of scant interest but would later find it of more importance. We walked, perhaps two to three miles more, along the lane and crossed a small bridge over a stream.

Holmes said, 'One would never imagine this being the same river Adur which emerges wide and salty at Shoreham.' I glimpsed a distant horse-drawn vehicle mercifully not raising the cloud of dust that would be normal for much of the year.

Soon I recognized the aged horse. 'See, Holmes, it's the cart, for I cannot refer to it as anything else, which collected us from the station. The poor animal walks no faster than a London policeman on his beat.'

Sure enough it was Mr Arthur Fox and his equipage. He touched his hat, though not in a subservient manner. 'Good morning, gentlemen. We meet again!'

Then he did something, I judged quite from instinct, that no servant or menial would dream of doing: he extended a hand, first to myself and then to Holmes. He had a good firm handshake to match his general manly style.

Holmes said, 'I notice you walk beside your horse instead of sitting in the driver's seat of your vehicle.'

Fox said, 'Why yes. It is almost yule-tide and I reckon the poor beast deserves a rest. I would have left him in his loose box until Boxing Day, but the truth is he enjoys a walk at his own pace; yet after so many years with the brougham his behaviour is rather nervous without it.'

I said, 'Upon my word, sir, you make him sound more like a pet than a beast of burden!'

He laughed, 'Wish that he were, Doctor. If I were wealthy he could have his own meadow and never want for anything for the rest of his days. But I must not detain you longer, my aunt is expecting me to visit her.'

We realized that it was high time we returned to the Manor if we were to catch even a late breakfast, so we walked beside him, keeping our pace down to that of the horse's, as he himself did.

When the horse stopped as we reached the old lady's cottage I realized that she must be Fox's aunt. But Holmes was much ahead of this small realization. He said, 'So your aunt is a Reynaud, Mr Fox, as indeed you are yourself. There is a certain likeness in your features to those of the subjects of the portraits upon the stairway at the Manor; also the fact that Fox is simply an English version of Reynaud cannot be a coincidence.'

He was a little taken aback by Holmes's statements, but not at all dismayed. 'Come Mr Holmes, Doctor, there is no earthly reason why my connection with the Reynaud menage should be a secret. But then here is my Aunt Mirelda who, I feel sure, will tell you rather more of our concerns than you might wish to hear!'

Soon we were seated within the cottage and Mirelda Reynaud was plying us with herb tea and home-made scones. Fox was right in that we were to hear much from her that did not concern us but wrong in the assumption that we would not find this to be of interest.

She said, 'I have two nephews, Gerald and Arthur here. When my dear husband Cedric Reynaud passed away last year he had made a will some time previously in favour of Gerald. However, when Gerald, after a series of escapades, finally brought disgrace upon us all, Cedric made a new will in favour of dear Arthur. I know that he drafted out the new will but he did it only a very short time before his death and we have never been able to find it. The authorities gave us a year to produce the new will. If it is not found within a few days Gerald will be master of Shaw Manor and on my death he will inherit all of the monies and investments of the Reynaud family.'

I enquired, 'But if the terms of the will are that you will not hand over the Manor to MacMillan yet and the monies not in your lifetime, why is he already ensconced in the Manor whilst you live in this cottage?'

She looked sad as she replied, 'When he asked to be able to use the Manor for a Christmas function I could find no reason to refuse him. After all, although all the servants have been kept on I have preferred to live in this cottage myself, for lone occupancy of the Manor is not very pleasing for an old lady. Here I am comfortable enough, especially as Arthur never fails to visit me each day.'

As soon as Arthur had left the room to fetch her a cushion, Mirelda Reynaud said to us, 'He is such a dear boy, so different from his cousin. When he suffered the loss of his business through no fault of his own he flatly refused my financial help and has started all over again from nothing.'

Holmes enquired, 'Dear lady, how long a period of time remains before MacMillan inherits, assuming that you are still unable to find the second will?'

She replied, 'About three months, Mr Holmes, but I have quite given up searching for it. Whilst I was still residing in the Manor I naturally made every effort to find where Cedric had stored it for safe keeping. The servants were wonderful, combing the whole building for it and of course they did not wish to have Gerald as a master.'

I could see that Holmes was on the point of enquiring if he might smoke, when the kind old lady sensed his craving for tobacco and produced a box of Turkish cigarettes. Holmes took one gratefully and I took one as well. Rather to my surprise Mirelda lit one herself.

The charming lady plied us with more tea and she and Arthur Fox treated us with every kindness, yet when she eventually asked a favour we got no feeling that we would have been treated differently had there been no favour to ask.

It was of course the obvious request. 'Do you think, Mr

Holmes, whilst you and your friend are staying at the Manor, you could keep an eye open and see if you can get some clue as to where that will might have been hidden . . .' She tailed off. 'You being a detective . . .'

Her voice started to shake as she bravely recommenced her oration. 'I am an old woman with perhaps a very short time left to me. It would be so wonderful if I could just live to see Arthur as the last of the Reynauds rather than that other scheming nephew of mine!'

Holmes gave the answer which I knew he would. He said, 'My dear Mrs Reynaud, you have my word upon it. Perhaps I can bring a certain skill to the task; a skill for which I have some slight reputation.'

I looked at him carefully and could see that he intended no irony. He was a man who took his own undoubted talent lightly. We left the cottage with a clear invitation to return.

Having shaken hands with Arthur Fox we strode back in the direction of Shaw Manor, by now far too late for breakfast. However, such triviality was far from our minds. We might, we felt, be not much nearer to discovering MacMillan's real reason for holding his yule-tide gathering and yet had collected another interested party, interested that is in our discoveries.

I had a feeling that the two matters, the seemingly trivial one and that of the missing will, were connected. I felt sure that Holmes had that same feeling. He was strangely silent as we passed through the imposing doorway and made for the fireplace. That glow which usually results in walking out of a winter chill and into the warmth of a well-heated room seemed to me to be absent.

I still felt that chill when our host greeted us. 'Holmes, Watson, it is no longer too early to wish you a Merry Christmas!'

vial shade of the kind that haunted Scrooge, MacMillan threw wide his arms in a gesture of seasonal geniality.

Holmes was unsmiling as he responded, 'But perhaps still a little early to wish you everything you deserve in the new year to come?'

MacMillan was silent for a moment, the mask of bonhomie slowly dropping from his ample features.

Then he said, 'Ah, the new year! Let us see what the yule-tide brings with it first, sir.'

Quickly he resumed his jolly façade, but he had been close to raising his guard.

Our host almost dropped his jolly persona again somewhat later in the day. We were gathered in the large room following a splendid Christmas Eve luncheon. The cold fowl and chilled Rhine wine had been dealt with and we each stood with a spirit glass, the big log fire forming its usual focal point.

There was a disturbance coming from the direction of the entrance hall. Suddenly two men, still sporting their greatcoats and hard felt hats, burst into the room, one of them brandishing a paper document. He spotted MacMillan and walked over thrusting the paper all but under his nose.

He spoke in an unrefined rasping voice. 'George Foster, alias Gerald MacMillan, I have been instructed by my employers, Lovelace, Jones and Lovelace, being solicitors of Holborn, London, to serve upon you this writ. I am also instructed to tell you that if I do not receive from you the sum of £258.8s.6½d, my colleague and I are to stay upon these premises, maintained at your expense, until this matter is resolved. This means, guv'nor, that you will need to give us three squares each a day, plus a-payin' of our wages, namely one pound each per day.'

Holmes breathed to me, 'Upon my word, the bailiffs! This pantomime grows in its authenticity by the minute. I wonder when Dan Leno will make his entrance.'

MacMillan's other guests were shocked into silence. The servants ceased in the surliness of their expressions save one, whom I guessed to be MacMillan's valet and as such was probably connected to our host rather than to the Manor. Indeed his had been the only hand raised to prevent the entrance of the intruders. He stood by MacMillan now, seeming to fume with rage. As for our host, his usually ruddy face had assumed an ashen hue. He stood there, like a broken man who, thus disgraced in public, knew not what to do. He fumbled with the paper and then swiftly ushered the shifty pair from the room.

After a momentary shocked silence there was a babble of concerned conversation among the guests.

Harding said to Holmes, 'Surely his game, whatever it might be, is up now, Holmes?'

But my friend said, 'He is resourceful, Harding. He may wriggle his way out of this yet.'

Yes, and sure enough he did. MacMillan returned to the big room with the two bailiffs, an arm around each of them. He led the pair of them over to the fireplace and called for his man to bring them liquid refreshment. Then raising his own glass to them he addressed the company in general.

'Ladies and gentlemen, allow me to introduce two more of our guests who will be with us for Christmas. Mr Roger Miles and Mr George Sutcliffe. Both are professional actors and when I invited them for Christmas, recruiting them in much the same manner as I did your good selves, it occurred to me to play a little seasonal prank and I beguiled them into playing the parts of broker's men, here to collect monies due. I thought it might provide a little bit of a thrill, followed by a good laugh.'

Aye and a good laugh there was, starting with a polite chortle from Bowser and a snort from Miss Finch, building to general laughter of a more open kind.

Holmes said to us both softly, 'Incredible. He has saved the day for himself by making a pact with the devil, so to speak. It will not have taken too large a bribe to buy off these two until after the holidays. No doubt they will play the parts that he has so suddenly and resourcefully invented for them and enjoy the hospitality as well.'

Mrs Glastonbury confirmed Holmes's words by saying to me, 'Isn't Mr MacMillan a scream? Who but he could have thought of introducing thespians to enact that little drama? Do you know, I all but believed they were real at first. I wonder what other surprises the dear man has in store for us?'

She giggled excitedly as she rejoined her husband by the fire.

Mr Coldharbour was congratulating the two intruders themselves. 'Capital performance, my dear sirs. Tell me, what play are you currently appearing in?'

One of the rascals touched his nose, winked an eye and said, '*The Merchant of Venice*. We are 'ere for our pound of flesh, haw, haw!'

There was general merriment and whilst their appearance must have dismayed MacMillan he had transformed a tragedy into a successful farce. I wondered, as had Mrs Glastonbury, what other surprises lay in store.

CHAPTER THREE

That day before Christmas was packed with entertainment for the guests of Mr Gerald MacMillan. A superb dinner was followed by an entertainment to rival that of the night before. First a lady who played sweetly upon the musical glasses, followed by a Mr Finlay Dunne who was very amusing at the piano with songs, clever humour and funny stories, but all in good taste.

All save Holmes seemed delighted with the entertainment. He sat through it, eyes closed and with a rather strained expression, especially when the lady with the musical glasses rubbed the rim of one tumbler which she had evidently over- or under-filled.

But he brightened up when our host announced, 'Another from my collection of the wonders of modern invention, the Magic Lantern. Of course in its basic use the showing of slides goes back many years. But at the end of this demonstration you will see actual moving pictures!'

The more usual views of the Holy Land beloved of Sunday school principals had been replaced by street scenes from London, Paris and New York, the seven wonders of the world and well-known personalities. MacMillan's valet operated the contraption whilst his master announced and commented upon each slide in a brisk, professional manner, even embellishing some of them with a pianistic background. George Robey drew the biggest laugh of recognition, whilst our own dear Queen Victoria drew applause. There were a few sniffles at some of the sentimental depictions in which dogs and children were featured.

Finally came the promised moving pictures in which the sun actually seemed to rise and a battleship sank into the vast deep of the ocean in an all too realistic manner. I confessed afterwards to not knowing quite how it had been managed but Holmes, who had nodded knowingly during the performance said, 'Very ingenious, my dear Watson.'

All of the guests evidently enjoyed it all, though the professor's wife was heard to remark to Holmes, 'Her Majesty, of course, and dear Mr Irving by all means; but George Robey? Why, he was actually depicted wearing a woman's dress, whilst there was another slide showing a young woman wearing breeches!'

Holmes said, 'Come, dear lady. It takes all kinds to make a world.'

In reply she snapped, 'Not in Cheltenham, it doesn't!'

Although MacMillan's huge Christmas tree had been decorated much earlier than tradition would have decreed, he had left it until this very eve of Christmas to light its candles. This had been done whilst we were in the drawing-room enjoying the entertainment, and with the oil lamps lowered it presented quite a picture for the guests as they entered the big room.

'Oh, what a picture!' Miss Finch was absolutely thrilled by the sight of the exciting-looking little packages, glistening and shimmering in the candlelight.

Holmes informed me, 'It was lit by the second footman, Watson.'

I said, 'Do you think the protocol is that exact?'

He chuckled. 'It would appear so, from the candlewax upon his right sleeve!'

Our host, at first to our surprise, suddenly gave an order for the heavy living-room curtains to be opened. But it soon became clear that he had done this that we might see the heavy fall of snow which gave that éclat to the yule-tide scene.

Then I thought MacMillan surpassed himself as a showman as members of his staff in costumes of an earlier day and age paraded outside the window, singing *The Holly and the Ivy* in rough but not unpleasing vocalization.

Our host had indeed spared no effort to ensure a Christmas Eve that we would never forget. Indeed it had occurred to me at this point that the yule-tide itself might be somewhat anti-climactic. Looking back now upon the events that were to follow I would that this had been so.

Christmas Day itself dawned bright, though the cold was intense and the snow lay deep and crisp. A pre-breakfast walk shook away all our cobwebs and gave us quite an appetite for the splendid fare which awaited us. There, on a side-table, were rashers of bacon, fat pork sausages, kedgeree, fried potato croquettes and of course toasted homemade bread and rich farmhouse butter.

Even Holmes managed to eat more heartily than I had known him to for a long time. We sat at a table with the two 'actors' who according to MacMillan were merely playing their parts as 'broker's men'. I teased them by asking about their recent histrionic activities (there being a lingering doubt in my mind).

Miles answered my insinuating enquiry, 'Oh yes. Mr Sutcliffe and I have just finished a long run in *Macbeth*.'

Then Sutcliffe chipped in, and started to quote from the play, 'Is this a dagger I see in my hand?'

After they had finished their second or third plateful, they wished us good day and left.

As soon as they were out of earshot, Holmes asked, 'Is your question answered, Watson, for I know your trusting nature and desire to give the benefit of any doubt.'

I said, 'Well, Holmes, they looked us straight in the eye and quoted from *Macbeth* in quite a facile manner . . . do you not think it possible that they are actors?'

He laughed. 'Oh come, Watson. I never dreamt that they might be thespians at any point in time. Did you notice their complexions? The daily application of grease paint and cocoa butter makes for clean and open pores, which our two friends certainly do not have. There are other signs; for instance, did you notice their cuffs?'

I said, 'Well, I admit that I noticed that they both had very slightly frayed jacket sleeves, but one must not be snobbish, Holmes; acting is not exactly a highly paid occupation for most thespians.'

He nodded. 'True, and I am no snob, Watson. But my experience of actors has shown me that they are very resourceful people. Your actor with a frayed cuff would treat it with soap and cut it clean with a razor. But our conversation, or rather your conversation, with them of the last few minutes must have made it clear even to you that they are imposters. Have you ever heard an actor who pronounced the name of the play *Macbeth*, even in casual conversation? It is the most important theatrical taboo. An actor would have referred to it as "The Scottish play", and would never quote from the text of the play except in actual rehearsal! Oh no, they are genuine bailiffs, I'll be bound.'

After breakfast we repaired to the big room where extra logs had been placed on the fire against the intense cold of the day. A more seasonal yule-tide I had never experienced nor have I since, but the good day had a sting in its tail to make it a Christmas that I would never want to experience again. However, I am getting too far ahead with my story and must come to things in their correct sequence.

Each guest received a little gift from Gerald MacMillan, myself included. These were just small, simple, but well-chosen items; lavender water for the ladies, an almanac for the professor and a cigarette case for Mr Coldharbour. Mr Bowser got a box of golf balls, friend Harding a splendid watch chain, whilst I received a box of cigars. Sherlock Holmes was the only one of us who did not receive a gift. Those of us who had, of course, were anxious to bestow our gratitude upon Mr MacMillan. He waved away our thanks and withdrew with dignity and modesty, making his exit amid a chorus of thanks.

I opened my box of cigars and decided it would be only polite to offer them round among the male company. Each accepted, save Holmes, who very pointedly produced for himself a case containing Egyptian cigarettes. I knew that he would have preferred a pipe but there were of course ladies present.

Later, Harding singled us out and said, 'Mr Holmes, what do you make of the fact that he pointedly left you out at the present distribution? Did he forget to get you something, or has he decided to make some kind of point?'

Holmes said, 'He has not forgotten me, and he would not make this pointed omission if it were not part of some plan, innocent or otherwise. No, my present is yet to come and will be presented with that showman's air that he has.'

Then about five minutes later Gerald MacMillan reappeared, smiling like a Cheshire cat.

He said, 'Mr Holmes, I have not forgotten your Christmas gift! I have invited a friend of yours to spend the day with us!'

Holmes worked hard upon his cigarette before he replied,

'I have only one friend, Mr MacMillan, and he stands beside me in the person of Dr John H. Watson. You have probably discovered the presence of a colleague, for you would not refer to my brother Mycroft as a friend. Yes, I have one or two colleagues but only one who wears size twelve boots, the toes of which can be seen protruding from the bottom of the curtains on that alcove beside the fireplace.'

He turned to me and said, 'You can judge a boot size even from their toes, Watson.'

Then he said, 'Do come out of that alcove, Inspector Lestrade. You must be quite stiff from standing still for such a long time.'

Lestrade emerged from behind the curtain, giving us both a rueful smile.

He said, 'Mr Holmes, a merry Christmas, and to you, Doctor! I was surprised to be invited to this Christmas party, I can tell you, but I might have known that you were behind it all. I was spending Christmas all on my own at the Grand Hotel in Brighton, my family being away and my work having made it impossible for me to go with them to Scotland.'

We introduced Harding to the inspector and the four of us decided to take a stroll, ostensibly to sharpen our appetites for Christmas lunch. Far from presenting any sort of offence to our intent, our host appeared quite happy to see us go off together. But then, I considered, had he not wished us to consort with Lestrade he would scarcely have gone out of his way to invite the man from Scotland Yard to his Christmas party.

We took it in turns to tell Lestrade of the events of the last few days. Long experience of the inspector had shown me that, although a plodder and sometimes lacking a little in imagination, he was a first-class detective perhaps head and shoulders above his colleagues. Holmes, I knew, despite sometimes dealing with him in a somewhat ironic manner, had yet the best of regard for Lestrade.

He had once said to me, 'Watson, when all the thinking and scheming have been done and the due process of law is essential, then Lestrade is your man. Straight as a die, the right sort to have in your corner. That abrasive quality that he has when dealing with me is only a shield to cover his frustration when I have noticed some trifle, one which he has ignored, which proves to be vital to an investigation.'

Certainly I had then and have yet vivid memories of that co-operation and backing-up that Lestrade gave to Holmes, partly responsible for my friend being able to bring that extraordinary case to a successful conclusion.

I had half expected the inspector to take MacMillan at face value and perhaps say, 'Anything wrong with a generous chap wanting people around him at Christmas?'

Instead, however, he said, 'You did the right thing to take this matter seriously, Mr Holmes. There is something rather rum here, I agree. After all, he must know how odd it will seem to ourselves yet appears not to be concerned by this. Come, gentlemen, you have a head start on me and I would like to have your considered opinions. Mr Holmes, you must have formed some kind of a theory by now . . . you are famous for theories!'

Holmes was taking full advantage of our stroll to puff away at a particularly disreputable clay pipe, and spoke between sharp intakes and exhalations of breath, producing smoke to rival that from a locomotive.

He spoke, when at last he did so, in a rather concerned manner. 'My dear Lestrade, I believe I have part of the answer, yet cannot seem to grasp the entire picture. It may be that more of the drama will need to unfold to make any kind of clear vista possible. Let us then consider all that has happened; you must forgive me, Inspector, if I repeat some details with which we have already made you familiar, but I feel that it is a good time for me to speak aloud concerning that which we have learned. First there is the matter of the invitations themselves. Directly and indirectly he has invited nine complete strangers for Christmas, or, as he likes to call it, yule-tide festivities. The nine have in fact become ten with the inclusion of your good self, Lestrade. You were the only person known to him by reputation to be invited, for Watson and I, though of some notoriety, were totally unexpected by our host. It is true that he started a little when we made our entrance, but his recovery was swift enough to show me that he did not consider us a hindrance for his plans. All of his guests, ourselves included, have one thing in common; we are all of us extremely respectable. He chose respectable-seeming contacts; Harding, Miss Finch and Mr Bowser would clearly move in conservative circles. I think that as a custodian of the law, Inspector, you would be likely to believe a statement made by any of the guests at Shaw Manor. MacMillan's plans may include his depending upon this pristine quality. We came here knowing a little of MacMillan's background and since then we have learned enough to know that he is financially embarrassed; witness the bailiff's putting in a surprise appearance with his handling of the situation showing that we are dealing with an extremely plausible rogue. I do not believe that he particularly wished us to be aware of his aunt who resides in the gate house and the fact that we have learned the details of his uncle's will might well be a slip-up on his part which, if able to, we must take full advantage of.'

There was a pause so long that Lestrade felt obligated to

speak. 'Yet there has been no crime committed and we have no reason to believe, despite his background, that MacMillan is anything more than an eccentric. After a career in petty crime could he not be anxious to make amends to his fellow men?'

Holmes reacted to his words with surprising animation. 'No crime as yet, but crime is involved, I feel sure of it, and I hope that it is of such a nature that it can be prevented rather than detected after it has taken place. Despite his joviality the host at Shaw Manor is hard-pressed and I believe the seemingly trifling sum mentioned by the bailiffs may be just the tip of the iceberg. The good Mirelda Reynaud tells us that, with the new will being lost, MacMillan will inherit within months, but no monies for possibly some years, and his debts may be so pressing that he has not years, months or even weeks before financial ruin overtakes him. I think this is the most interesting aspect of our puzzle.'

After a really splendid Christmas luncheon, the goose served with herbs and aspic amid slices of roast beef was followed by a Christmas pudding of enormous dimensions. In exploring my portion of the pudding with a fork in case the old tradition of the silver coin had been respected I was amazed to find a tiny gold piece of the kind which can be hung from a watch chain. Then later we sat around the fire with glasses of brandy and a vast pile of extremely fine mince pies. Our host mingled with us all, with that air of joviality that was fast beginning to irritate me.

He eventually sidled over to Holmes and said, 'Mr Holmes, I have a favour to ask of you. Do you think that you could take a small present from me to my aunt at the keeper's house? I fear she might not be too happy to see me, due to this foolish family upset. But she might take this little package from you, and, who knows, she might even then be calm enough to accept it. There is another reason too. I want to be sure that she is safe and well. I know from observation that my wretched cousin Arthur calls upon her at about seven each evening. With all his faults he is I believe fond of her, but I don't want her to be entirely alone on Christmas Day.'

Holmes would have found it hard to refuse such a modest request and he quickly agreed to take the little package. I offered to go with him but he swiftly told me with his gimlet eyes to stay where I was.

MacMillan said, 'Perhaps Inspector Lestrade would also like a short walk, Mr Holmes?'

Lestrade rose from his chair and assented. Our host thanked them both and then asked the inspector, 'What is the time by your watch, Inspector? I believe my clock is a little slow.'

He glanced up at the dial on the grandfather clock which stood in the corner.

Lestrade studied his watch and said, 'Why, sir, it is just two minutes to four, your clock is correct within a few seconds.'

When Holmes and Lestrade had departed I managed to snatch a short converse with Harding. 'What do you make of that?'

He replied, 'I don't know, but he seemed pleased for the inspector to go to the keeper's house with Mr Holmes. And did you notice how he so pointedly asked Lestrade for the time when I am sure he knew that his clock was accurate enough?'

I nodded. 'We must keep an eye open for anything unusual so that we can report to Holmes when he returns.'

For it had occurred to me that MacMillan might be about to take some step that he would rather Holmes did not observe.

It seemed to me that Holmes and Lestrade were gone for about an hour, with the grandfather clock striking five just a minute after their return.

MacMillan naturally enquired concerning their errand, asking, 'I hope you wished my aunt a happy Christmas from me?'

Lestrade nodded. 'The good lady was not too forthcoming and there is no message for us to deliver.'

Holmes added, 'But at least she has not returned your gift.'

MacMillan shrugged in a fairly jovial fashion, saying, 'Well, you did what you could and I am grateful.'

From that time on MacMillan was the life and soul of the party, *his* party. He distributed gifts at first in his own persona and later, having slipped behind the screen at the side of the alcove at the end of the room, he reappeared in the guise of Santa Claus. It was a splendid and expensive-looking outfit in red velvet, with fur-trimmed boots and sleeves. He wore a splendid silver-white beard which appeared to hook onto his ears, this fact partially hidden by a red velvet beret, also trimmed with white fur. I noticed that it was about half past six when he stood on the platform and led the company in the singing of carols and other seasonal songs.

He had a good voice, robust tenor I think you would call it, and considering that he did not use any sort of musical accompaniment seemed to stay in key. Every few minutes he would dive behind the screen and emerge again with fresh favours and streamers to toss among us. This carol singing and prize distribution continued for about twenty minutes until it was most dramatically interrupted by a frantic banging at the front door.

The butler, who answered the door, was pushed roughly aside by Arthur Fox, who shouted with desperate urgency, 'My aunt, Mirelda, has been murdered!'

Lestrade was the first on his feet and he hastened to Fox's side, attempting to calm the obviously dazed and distraught man.

He laid a hand on his shoulder and said, 'My dear sir, calm yourself and please explain exactly what has occurred.'

Then, turning to the rest of the company, he said, 'I must ask the rest of you to also keep calm and to stay just where you are for the moment. I will accompany Mr Fox to the scene of this alleged crime, and Mr Holmes, Dr Watson, please may I depend on you both to keep everything organized here?'

Fox and Lestrade departed together in some haste and, after they had left, a buzz of amazed conversation pervaded the room.

I remarked quietly to Holmes, 'I am surprised that the inspector did not ask you to accompany himself and Fox to the keeper's house.'

But he waved this remark aside. 'Oh come. Lestrade, as the only person present with official status would want to observe the scene of the crime, if crime it is, without my amateur muddling, as he would call it. This is right and proper. However, I am slightly surprised that he did not ask you as a medical man to go with him, in case you could have possibly saved her if only wounded, or at the very worst to declare life to be extinct. But I'm sure he will soon have the local police upon the scene and all the official protocol will be observed.'

Meanwhile, Gerald MacMillan was very slowly and deliberately removing his Santa Claus costume, boots and beard to reveal that he was wearing his evening dress clothes beneath them.

Finally, as the hat was removed, he crossed over to us and said, 'God, what a tragedy. Who on earth would want to kill my poor dear aunt?'

I replied as comfortingly as I could, 'Come, sir, perhaps Mr Fox is mistaken. Perhaps she has merely fainted or, at worst, suffered a seizure.'

He said, 'I pray to God that you are right, sir, but if not I avow that I will see that her killer is brought to justice if it is the last thing that I do!'

Then MacMillan's voice became, for him, just a trifle subdued as he said, 'Mr Holmes, if you are able to apprehend the beast who has done this dreadful thing you will not find me ungrateful, sir. Why, when I think of that poor dear sweet old lady, so kind to everyone she came in contact with, being attacked by a madman, it brings me close to tears.'

He took a large cambric square from inside his jacket and dabbed at his eyes with it prior to blowing his nose with an exhibitionist's flourish, before he continued, 'He must have been a madman, must he not?'

Holmes turned to me and whispered, 'What a superb actor, Watson. He expects that he would have been a suspect had his alibi not been so strong.'

Harding drew Holmes and me to one side and whispered, 'Have we at last found the true answer to the mystery of our host being so anxious to invite us here?'

Holmes said, 'Come, we are ahead of ourselves, Harding. Let us receive confirmation of the true situation before jumping to conclusions.'

But it occurred to me that he had hit the right note.

Then, when Lestrade and Fox returned with the inspector backing up Fox's claims, I felt sure that there was something in Harding's theory.

Lestrade addressed the company in clipped official tones. 'Now, ladies and gentlemen, if I might have your full and undivided attention I will give you some idea of the event which has led to the uncertainty of the recent past. At about seven of the clock Mr Arthur Fox discovered the lifeless body of his aunt, Mrs Mirelda Reynaud. He found her sitting in an armchair with her back to the open french window of her sitting room, with the back of her head caved in, seemingly the result of a blow from a heavy instrument such as an iron bar. Life was so obviously extinct that I had no reason to send for you, Dr Watson, and whilst I will later value your theories, Mr Holmes, I have at this moment no official freedom to allow anyone to inspect the scene of the crime. I have sent a boy who was in the lane for the local police who will no doubt arrive shortly and will take charge. As an off-duty police inspector it is merely my place to preserve any evidence and await official orders.'

Holmes and I exchanged glances; there was no need now for any sort of whispered conversation.

My friend said, 'Inspector, perhaps I might voice a few of my theories to help pass the time before the Henfield police arrive. By the way, does the force involve just a single constable or a pair of them?'

Lestrade replied with great dignity, 'I believe there are two of them, but one of them will be a sergeant, and in any case he will send to Lewes for reinforcements and instructions.'

Holmes nodded. He lit a Turkish cigarette which caused Miss Finch to cough.

He addressed the assembled persons. 'We are all the

guests of Mr Gerald MacMillan, a seeming philanthropist, a sort of nineteenth-century Kriss Kringle, so aptly attired as he stands before us at this very moment. I believe we were all recruited in a similar way and most of us have enjoyed our Christmas treat far too much to question its purpose.'

MacMillan started, then said, 'Mr Holmes, I had believed that Dr Watson and yourself had been enjoying my hospitality as much as anyone here. Why, when I asked Mr Harding to bring two friends I had not expected an investigator and his Boswell, but I was happy that you could join us. Please do not give me reason to regret my earlier feelings. Miss Finch, you and your friends have enjoyed yourselves, I'll be bound . . .'

There was a chorus of assent, indeed from the whole company save ourselves and Harding, the latter remarking, 'I found the invitation strange, sir, which caused me to invite Sherlock Holmes in his official capacity.'

MacMillan looked theatrically hurt and said, warmly, 'Why, sir, you have quite dented my faith in human nature; what a singularly ungrateful fellow you have turned out to be. Obviously in my generosity I am my own worst enemy and have been clutching a viper to my bosom! I feel sure that my other guests are as horrified as I am myself at your suspicions about my honest hospitality. What possible reason could I have for filling my fine house with guests, and in any case what has any of this to do with the terrible tragedy which has occurred? Have you no feelings for a man who has just been bereaved by the loss of a dear close relative?'

There followed a murmur of sympathetic assent which changed to stifled astonishment as Holmes rose to his feet to reply.

'Having carried out certain investigations into your past and aspects of your career as a confidence trickster I could not claim that I came here with a completely open mind, though to be completely fair I was willing to give you the benefit of the doubt. You were taken aback when Dr Watson and I were introduced by Mr Harding, but I'll grant that you made a swift recovery, perhaps realizing that our inclusion in your gathering would add credence to your plans.'

Our host was still trying to preserve his calm as he all but snapped, 'Plans, sir? What *are* these mysterious plans?'

To quote an ancient adage, one could have heard a pin drop, before Holmes replied, in serious tones, 'You invited these people to your home for Christmas because you wanted to use them . . . yes, use them in order to provide you with an alibi. For this reason you chose this method of inviting near strangers, whilst making pretty sure that they would be respectable gentlefolk in order to add credence to their words regarding yourself and your movements. Indeed, the presence of Watson and me, you felt upon reflection, would make your scheme the stronger.'

I must give MacMillan full credit for the continued bravado with which he dealt with the accusation of Sherlock Holmes.

He now adopted a slight tone of irony. 'What possible reason could I have, Mister Detective, for this strategy which you suggest?'

Holmes was deadly serious now as he said, 'In order to carry out a brutal murder whilst evidently in the full view of a number of persons.'

This statement brought Inspector Lestrade to his feet. He raised an admonishing finger as he said, 'Steady on there, Mr Holmes. Take great care in making such an accusation. Remember that you are in the presence of a police inspector and whilst I am not, as yet anyway, assigned to this case I could hardly conceal your accusing words from officialdom.'

Holmes nodded sagely. 'Do not worry, Inspector. I can substantiate my accusation which is not merely theoretical.'

Lestrade said, 'Please remember that there will be other suspects, one at least, and completely without any sort of alibi. Mr Fox, for instance, claimed to have discovered the body of the poor lady but we have only his word that she was already dead when he called on her at about seven of the clock. Of course we know that you called on her yourself at four, the time having been pointed out to us by Mr MacMillan.'

There was, I felt, a tiny touch of irony in Lestrade's voice too, though perhaps only one who knew him well would notice it.

He continued, 'I believe you mentioned to me earlier today, Holmes, that without the discovery of a disputed second will left by the lady's late husband, Mr MacMillan would inherit everything, including this house, and within a few months at that. Why would he wish to kill the lady under such circumstances?'

Holmes paused and, throwing good manners to the wind, took out and filled his pipe.

However, he did not light it before he spoke. 'Because his financial pressures are too great for him to wait even a short period, let alone risk the discovery of the second will. The two so-called actors, in fact bailiffs, are but the tip of a huge iceberg of debt. Gerald MacMillan knew that her death was the only alternative to, at worst the debtors' prison, at best public disgrace. As for his cousin, Arthur Fox, he has no motive whatsoever, benefiting not at all from his aunt's death. She was in fact his only ally and he was more than fond of her.'

Fox nodded dumbly, and MacMillan, or Reynaud as we knew him to be, was also silent for perhaps ten seconds. His guests muttered among themselves. Then MacMillan played his last and, as he viewed it, his trump card. He spoke in calculated tones.

'Very clever, Mr Holmes, but all quite fictitious. I will grant that you could construct a scenario which might make that to which you have entertained us to seem to be so. But I tell you that this evidence is quite circumstantial, an amalgam of wild theoretical fantasy and pure coincidence. I am innocent of this dreadful crime, one of which I am incapable and, what is more, I can prove my innocence for, by your own admission, Holmes, I have the perfect alibi, having been here in full view of my guests during the entire period which is in doubt. It was not, as you have suggested, my intention to give myself some sort of alibi for a crime which I could not even suspect was happening. But whilst the benevolence in which I have indulged myself was simply part of my character I am happy that by chance it has proved me innocent of that which you have the audacity to accuse me. As for you, Dr Watson, what price "The Great Sherlock Holmes Libel Action" for your *Strand Magazine* readers? No, the company present, yourselves included Holmes, Watson, Inspector Lestrade, will be forced to swear upon oath that I have not left your sight for more than a few seconds at a time since four this afternoon. I need say no more until the police arrive, but I defy you to prove that my words are false, Mr Meddler Holmes!'

At last he had lost his temper, but my friend remained calm as he listened to MacMillan's tirade.

Then at last Holmes spoke his piece. 'You were seemingly within sight of the company during the whole of the period in question.'

Lestrade interrupted, rather prematurely I felt, 'But Mr Holmes, you surely do not question the evidence of a dozen pairs of eyes as suggested by your use of the word seemingly?'

There was again a good deal of muttering among those present which subsided as Holmes recommenced speaking. 'Inspector, I do not question that everyone present may believe that MacMillan was present during the whole of the time in question, but they are forgetting certain points. To begin with, he spent a good deal of that time disguised as Santa Claus, complete with a hat and face-enveloping beard. Watson, would you be so kind as to don the Santa Claus outfit right down to the beard, hat and boots?'

I did as I was asked and it was easily accomplished within perhaps half a minute. I stood upon the little platform, taking up a similar stance to that which had been adopted by our host.

Holmes turned to Lestrade and asked, 'Would you know that Watson was not MacMillan in that costume?'

Lestrade shook his head, 'Not really, aside from the colour of his eyes, and the fact that there is perhaps an inch between their heights.'

Holmes nodded and said sharply, 'Quite so, but suppose a person with the same height and eye pigmentation had been involved?'

The inspector said, 'Then I would say that it could be hard to tell a difference, particularly if not expecting Santa Claus to be anyone else, having seen him put on the costume.'

Holmes smiled in triumph. 'Of course, and I will introduce you to Santa's double!'

He threw himself into sudden action, diving behind the screen at the side of the platform and returning with another person wearing an exactly similar costume to the one we had been experimenting with. This new Santa Claus was an exact *doppelgänger* of the old one! He was the same height as MacMillan and had the same eye coloration as well as their build being extremely similar.

Holmes asked. 'Would you have known that this was not Gerald MacMillan?'

I had to be fair and said, 'Come, Holmes, his voice would have given him away. Perhaps this person, whoever he may be, could speak a few words?' The figure in the red costume said, 'I am Martins, Mr MacMillan's valet. As you can hear, however, we may look alike in these outfits but our voices are quite different. My master is a perfectionist, he had me "in the wings" so to speak, in case he should damage or otherwise render his costume in need of a change. They are quickly donned and removed so my easiest way to keep the spare costume and accessories together was to wear them!'

Unlikely, but perfectly logical. I looked to Holmes for some flaw in the explanation. I doubted that he could find it but in so doubting I did my friend's deductive ability a disservice.

Holmes explained, 'Behind the screen is one of the marvels of modern science; Edison's voice-machine which MacMillan used as a means of entertainment for us all a night or two back. Watson, please remove that ridiculous costume and then step behind the screen and tell me what you find.'

It took only seconds to remove the costume and having done so I stepped behind the screen and examined the machine. It had as before a cylinder mounted upon it and Holmes called to me to place the lever with its needle into the groove and turn the switch which operated the spring motor.

After a little experiment I managed to get the machine working and there came forth the sound of MacMillan's voice, singing a yule-tide carol; from MacMillan himself there came no sound at all.

Holmes, like some scientific professor in charge of an experiment, said, 'You see, our host had only to step behind the screen at a suitable point in time, start the machine and have his deputizing thespian step out with the sack of gifts (the fetching of which was the excuse for his momentary absence) and by mouthing the words of the carols convince the guests that there had been no change. MacMillan could then have very easily found time to slip away and commit the crime, so artfully planned, and return to change places with his valet-double before this cylinder ceased playing. I noticed that the machine was especially adapted to play a longer cylinder than is usual. I examined it closely last night when all but I were slumbering . . . yes, even you, Watson!'

MacMillan at this point said nothing. I broke the silence by asking, 'I suppose Martins was the only confederate, for I feel sure that the staff in general would, any of them, have informed upon this monster had they had an inkling?'

Holmes nodded. 'Yes, that is so, I believe. It took MacMillan but a few minutes to run across the grounds and surmount the hedge to enter the keeper's house garden. There he picked up the iron bar which was lying by the French window. He had only to open this and bludgeon the poor old lady who sat dozing with her back to him. He would have done his ghastly deed and made his return to Shaw Manor in the fastest possible time. To make his repeat exchange with Martins in the shortest possible time was the only problematical aspect of his plan. Finding his victim so tragically neatly arranged for his purpose was his bonus. Inspector, even in the absence of the official police I feel that it would be your duty to restrain Mr MacMillan even if you risk breaking some bye-law. In fact, if you do not do so I will collar the blackguard myself.'

What happened next took us all by surprise. MacMillan suddenly drew a small pocket revolver from the inside of his dinner-jacket and clapped it to Holmes's head. My friend may have been and still is the finest boxer of his weight in England, but he stood no chance in this situation. Even had I been carrying my service revolver, which I was not, I would have been hard put to intercede without risking Holmes's life.

The company in general, even Lestrade, were forced to watch MacMillan frogmarch Holmes backwards watching like a whole group of rabbits being mesmerised by a well-fed weasel. Martins ran ahead of them and opened the doors that would facilitate a fast exit.

MacMillan shouted, as we helplessly watched, 'Don't try to follow us or your world-famous detective will get it right through the brain. Yes, and I won't hesitate to blow any of *you* to kingdom come either. Remember, I have nothing to lose!'

We heard doors slam after them as they left Shaw Manor through the rear of the building. After a few seconds Lestrade, Harding and I bade the others to stay put and then risked following in the wake of Holmes and his captors. When we reached the rear grounds of Shaw Manor I immediately wished that our walks and explorations of the past few days had included this area. Alas, it had not and the grounds were mostly of a closely wooded nature. Even where there were no trees there were shrubs and huge weeds, long bereft of the attentions of scythe or sickle. It was impossible to find any sign of where or at which point they had disappeared into the undergrowth. It was dark, of course, but Lestrade seemed to have eyes like a hawk. After sending Harding to scan the front of the manor, to be sure that they had not doubled back, he started to creep along on his hands and knees like some Indian scout, looking for buckled grasses and broken bushes.

At this point the official police arrived in the persons of Sergeant Fairbrother and Constable Jenkins. Lestrade tried to present them with some sort of thirty-second version of what had occurred; but what with the murder, the method of the discovery of the murderer and the abduction of Holmes they became more and more confused by the second.

But one good thing came out of the arrival of the police. Sergeant Fairbrother had a lamp attached to the belt which spanned his ample girth. This light at least was some help to Lestrade in his scout craft. Despite his good-natured banter with Holmes carried on for so many years concerning the abilities of the official force and the theorist, he had I knew the greatest possible respect for my friend and did not intend to allow him to be harmed if he could prevent it.

He grew tired of directing the illumination with the lamp attached to the sergeant. He grabbed at the lamp, releasing the belt and directing the beam himself, muttering, 'I have no time for niceties, Sergeant. A man's life, and a good man's life at that, is at stake!'

As for myself, I sent Harding back to the house to fetch my revolver, and as we waited for his return for the first time I took in the enormity of what had happened, from the brutal killing of a fine old lady to the capture and imminent danger to the man whose only friend I was. I regretted so much now some of the harsh thoughts that had run through my mind when Holmes had denounced MacMillan and explained how, why and when he had managed to commit the crime. I had thought 'What is the use of Holmes having this great ability to solve mysteries if he could not prevent such a tragedy.'

With the information that he had evidently assembled why oh why had he not been able to predict and prevent? But now I realized that it was all too easy for me to be so wise after the event and I wished my friend present that I might apologize to him for an accusation never made. Mostly I just wished he were safely with us!

Maybe similar thoughts were running through Lestrade's not inconsiderable mind. He and Holmes had been colleagues of a sort during the whole period of my friendship with Sherlock Holmes. I say 'of a sort' because many of my readers might be tempted to interpret much that I have written regarding the association of the man from Scotland Yard and the sage of Baker Street. Thorns in each other's flesh? Maybe, but very small thorns they were and causing absolutely no ill-will in either direction.

Harding returned with my revolver to find that we had made no progress despite the aid of the policeman's lamp. By its light we would, I imagined, have discovered any trails of an obvious type. We were soon torn by brambles and had great difficulty in communication, afraid that the slightest sound might give away our presence in the undergrowth. But after about fifteen minutes of pointless exploration we decided that it could do little harm to confer in whispers. MacMillan had the advantage over us in that he knew his home territory. However, we had Fox with whom we consulted after having withdrawn from the undergrowth.

Lestrade asked him, 'How far does this undergrowth stretch before it reaches a road or the downs?'

Fox said, 'Several miles, and even then the undergrowth covers the lower part of the chalk slopes.'

Lestrade said, 'If only it were daylight, and if only there were a few more of us. As it is you who is the only one of us armed there is little point in our splitting up. In any case, time is our enemy.'

Sergeant Fairbrother spotted something on the ground in the light of the lamp. He gesticulated, pointing to a small rectangle of heavy buff paper, saying, 'I don't suppose there is any connection but a bus ticket is a bit unusual in these parts.'

Lestrade picked up the ticket and studied it under the lamp. He said, 'It could have just blown here from any-where.'

I asked if I might look at it and he passed it to me. I was at once intrigued by the print which gave its date and destination and I said, 'Inspector, this ticket is ten years out of date. What does that suggest?'

He shrugged. 'It's been lying around for a very long time?'

I felt that I was taking on the mantle of Holmes himself as I said, 'On the contrary, it is in remarkable, almost mint, condition, as if it had been issued only yesterday! Moreover, it has Oxford Circus as its destination. What is a ten-year-old bus ticket for Oxford Circus in pristine condition doing in the grounds of a country house in Sussex, thirty miles from that destination?'

Harding had caught my train of thought. He said, 'Could there be something special about this particular ticket?'

I nodded, although I doubt if the inclinations of my head were noticed. 'Exactly. It is probably a collector's item.

You see there is a misprint on the destination, it reads "Oxford Cicus", making it desirable to a collector.'

Lestrade said, rather stuffily, 'You mean that MacMillan is not only a rogue and a killer, but also collects bus tickets?'

I replied, 'No, but Holmes has recently placed a number of such items into the pockets of most of his jackets to use as bookmarks.'

I explained the circumstances, as quickly as I could, time being of the essence. Lestrade quickly understood and swept the beam of the sergeant's lamp around among the undergrowth to be rewarded eventually.

'Look, there's another of them!' Harding spotted another paper rectangle. This time it proved to be a five-year-old ticket from Finchley to Victoria. Within the next five minutes we found two others, of other dates and destinations. It was soon obvious that Holmes had been laying a trail with his collection of duplicates!

I had, of course, exhibited no brilliant deduction, for I alone among us had been possessed of the knowledge concerning Holmes's collection of tickets. He had thought them unimportant enough to use merely as bookmarks, but might live to rejoice that he had not simply thrown them away. Of course, that is just what he was doing at this very time, but in a calculated manner which told me that, although he was a captive, he had some freedom of movement, indicating that he was not tied or manacled.

As we followed the trail, Fox explained to me that his uncle had frequently disappeared into the dense undergrowth, sometimes not to be seen again for several hours.

I conveyed this information to Lestrade, who said, 'Perhaps we should then be watching for some concealed retreat, frequented by the late Mr Reynaud? Many wealthy men are eccentric and like to have some sort of private place where they can follow some pursuit or hobby, or just to be away from the cares of this world. What were his interests, Mr Fox?'

Arthur Fox replied, 'He was interested in photography, but otherwise he merely followed the pursuits of a normal English country gentleman.'

After several hours of quiet following of the trail we had collected a dozen bus tickets which would perhaps have taken only a few minutes for Holmes to distribute, our speed being dictated by the stealth which we needed to employ. We had to be quiet, and we had to keep the lamp shaded as much as possible. We disturbed a number of woodland creatures, several wood mice and an extremely mangey fox which startled us considerably as it leaped, panic-stricken, from beneath a bush, the luminosity of its eyes giving all of us quite a shock.

As the fox leapt away from us it emitted a rather characteristic cough, illustrating that it was in fact a vixen. This reminded me of an incident on the Scottish moors a few years earlier when Holmes and I had imitated that very sound in order to communicate secretly. Of course, the idea was not a novel one, because many aboriginal peoples, including tribes of American indians, have used bird calls and animal noises for locating each other when vocal speech would be unwise. I muttered to Lestrade that I could imitate that vixen's cough, perhaps giving Holmes some kind of inkling that we were in the vicinity.

The inspector enquired, 'If the fox has been in this locality for a while, might not Holmes be just as convinced that the noise is an animal?'

I said, 'No, we had a code before: three short coughs then a short silence followed by two more fox-like imitations.'

As we seemed to have reached the end of the trail, not

having sighted a bus ticket for ten minutes, he seemed of the opinion that my scheme could do no harm and might even bear fruit.

'Mind you,' said Lestrade, 'he won't be able to reply in like fashion will he, so we are just wasting our time in all probability. However, by all means try to warn Holmes that we are about.'

I gave my impersonation of the Vixen's cough three times, paused, and then repeated it twice. I was not, of course, expecting a response but felt that I could not just crouch in the undergrowth making no attempt to help my friend.

We watched and listened, and then I repeated the whole procedure in a more muted form, trying to give a naturalistic impression of a fox moving around in a normal manner. We crouched there for perhaps a further quarter of an hour before a reaction occurred, which I at first mistook for a flash of lightning.

We were, of course, startled and Harding was the first to speak. 'That flash was very close to us and certainly was not part of a storm.'

Lestrade agreed. 'There has been no thunder, however far away; I agree the flash was close and reminded me of a photographer's momentary illumination, caused by igniting that special powder that they use. Did you not mention that the late Mr Reynaud was interested in photography, Mr Fox?'

Arthur Fox agreed, saying, 'Is it possible that he had some kind of darkroom or laboratory concealed somewhere in this undergrowth?'

I found this rather surprising, 'Why would he wish to conceal his darkroom?'

Lestrade said, 'If you had been a policeman as long as I have, Doctor, nothing would surprise you!'

We moved forward cautiously now, extremely uncomfortably, on our stomachs, the close proximity of the flash making us fearful of discovery. We used the lamp but little, just for a second at a time.

Fox whispered, 'If it is indeed that they are hiding in some sort of concealed den it must surely be at least partly below ground.'

Lestrade grunted, almost inaudibly, 'Yet there must be some sort of aperture or window for us to have seen the flash.'

Then we caught a glimpse of a break in the undergrowth rather like a slot of the kind that one might have in a bird-watcher's hide. We were certain that we had found that which we were seeking, but of course we felt that only the first hurdle had been cleared.

We retreated a yard or two in order to decide on our next move.

Lestrade was all for throwing caution to the wind. 'There must be an entrance to this hide on its other side; I suggest that we go and find it and rely on the element of surprise in order to gain entrance by storming it.'

But Harding was in favour of caution. 'Two of us should go to the entrance, then if we do not gain anything or if the very worst should happen there will be someone to form a second column, or at the very least to send for reinforcements.'

Lestrade turned to Fairbrother. 'Sergeant, you are in charge, at least technically, so I would like you to decide upon our next move.'

Fairbrother said, 'I would like the Doctor to accompany me to the entrance, if indeed we find it. He has the only firearm amongst us and doubtless knows how to use it. Inspector, if you would stay here with the constable and the other gentlemen to form the reserve. I think the doctor could give his fox imitation to call us if required.'

Of course this conversation was delivered very quietly indeed, so I can only give the reader the roughest sketch of what was said.

Stealthily, the sergeant and I skirted around what we took to be the side of the hide. We dared not show the light, so we did this mainly through touch. Eventually, however, we took a chance on showing the shaded light just enough to gain some idea that we had reached the front of the construction. It proved to be a form of lean-to with a turfed roof, making it extremely hard to find even in day-light. But at last we found an entrance door, also disguised with tree bark and moss. We dared not even whisper lest we were heard and for some time we just crouched in the bracken and observed.

Then suddenly, after what seemed like an hour but was in fact probably only five minutes, the door opened and a figure loomed eerily in the aperture which the door had left.

I shone the light so that I might surprise MacMillan and his aide, raised my revolver and shouted, 'Raise your hands or I fire!'

A familiar voice responded, 'It is a seasonable evening is it not, my dear Watson?'

The unmistakable incisive tones of the world's only con-sulting detective continued, 'You need not worry about your service revolver for I have MacMillan's and he and his evil helper are within this concealed hut, trussed like chick-ens!'

'Holmes!' I shouted his name, then said, 'I was never so glad to see anyone in my life.' We shone the police lamp through the doorway and saw the evidence for ourselves, for there were MacMillan and his valet seated back-to-back with their hands bound behind them. Both glowered and muttered muted threats. I called out through the still cold night to inform Lestrade of what we had found.

I shouted, 'Inspector, you may approach. All is well!'

Soon they joined us and were as startled as we had been at the bizarre sight which greeted them. The sergeant wasted no time in producing the more official means of restraint and clamping them to the wrists of the two prisoners. He cautioned them and officially arrested the evil pair. He was singularly indifferent regarding the details of Holmes's turning of the tables and marched the prisoners away, leaving Holmes and me in the hut, with Lestrade and Harding, and with Fox a little undecided as to what he should do. Holmes, however, indicated that he should stay and hear his story . . .

Holmes commenced his narrative: 'As soon as MacMillan and his valet escaped, taking me with them into this dense undergrowth, I remembered that I had some of my omnibus tickets in the pocket of my dinner-jacket. I imagined that I could rely on you to spot and follow the trail, Watson, even if the police did not. To be fair, one would have to have known the history of the tickets to spot their significance. I guessed they had some kind of hide-out because they seemed to know just where they were going. Once inside, the unholy pair started to make plans to leave the district, if not the country. I imagine they had in mind to tie me up and slip away when they felt that the coast was clear. They fell out, of course, as rogues so often do. MacMillan was for shooting me when the time seemed right, but his valet, possibly fearful of this extra murder making it certain that they would both go to the gallows if caught, was all for tying me up and leaving me here. They argued about it for ages, quite unaware of the trail or thinking for one minute that any of you could be in the vicinity. Then I heard the cough of a vixen, and to my joy soon after your rather pathetic imitation of it, Watson.' He caught the flash of my eye even in the subdued lamp light! 'But, of course, this was as well because I realized at once that it was you and not our foxy friend. MacMillan obviously knows little concerning the night sounds of the Sussex countryside.'

Holmes paused irritatingly and lit one of his infernal Turkish cigarettes. He eventually continued, 'Then I had a stroke of good fortune. I had realized that this place had been used by a photographer, probably the late Mr Reynaud, as soon as I was brought into it. In fact I even noticed some photographic flash powder which had been spilled upon the floor. I quickly evolved a plan. I asked if I might smoke and fortunately MacMillan agreed that I may. He watched me like a hawk as I took out my case and vestas but did not anticipate my next move. Having lit the cigarette I dropped the still-glowing vesta upon some traces of the flash powder. This created a blinding flash which quite threw MacMillan off his guard and I was able to wrest the pistol from his hand with comparative ease. I made the valet tie up his master with some twine which I spotted on a shelf. It was easy enough for me to tie up the man-servant in his turn, considering his panic-stricken state. The rest you know, really, and as so often in the past I am indebted to you for your staunch support, my dear Watson. Without your animal impersonation and the thought that help was near I doubt that I would have had the confidence to plan my inspirational flash!'

After the police had departed with their prisoners we found a candle and once this was illuminated it gave us a good view of the interior of the hide, or darkroom as we now knew it to be. The only place where daylight, had there been any, would have filtered through was that slim rectangle which had given us the sight of the flash. I noted that there was a curtain which could be drawn to cover even this small aperture. We could see that even in strong daylight this primitive darkroom would have served its purpose well. There was a single shelf, upon which Holmes had found the twine, which also bore a number of chemical flasks, patently intended to contain various photographic developers and fixatives. Most of these were all but empty through evaporation. Below the shelf there was a badly stained sink with a tap which still seemed to function given a certain amount of encouragement. Below the sink was an area occupied by a rack, housing a number of negative-image glass full plates. We examined these carefully and discovered that they were for the most part recognizable as well-known views of the Sussex countryside.

Leaning against the opposite wall were a number of cameras, tripods and other pieces of photographic equipment, including one large mahogany camera, brass-bound and particularly impressive.

I think I expressed the general view when I said, 'One wonders why a man who owns such a large and impressive house with a group of well-built stables and other outbuildings should choose to build a make-shift darkroom in a most inconvenient thicket.'

Holmes said, 'Of course, Watson, this thought had occurred to me which is why I carefully examined the photographic plates beneath the sink lest their subject-matter should give some clue to a need for secrecy, but views of the downs and a few village streets would hardly need to be concealed. I was looking for something connected with espionage. However, we must remember that many people do observe a great deal of secrecy regarding their hobbies for fear of engendering mockery. I feel that the man who made these negatives need hardly have worried on that score. They are very fine examples of what is a comparatively new art, Watson, but art it is and there is little here that could not be admired. There is, however, one plate still in its holder over near the camera. The question is, has it already been exposed or is it yet to be used? If it has been exposed it will almost certainly prove to be yet another rustic idyll, but I will develop it, lest it should prove interesting.'

Here, then, was the difference between Sherlock Holmes and your run-of-the-mill investigator. Others would say, 'I will send the plate to be developed.' Lestrade, of course, had he been present in his official capacity, would not have dared to meddle with the plate even assuming he could have developed it. But Holmes just glanced at the row of bottles and decided that it was practical for him to proceed. Jack of all trades, yes, but Holmes, far from being master of none, was at least competent in most!

Holmes had soon found a lantern with red glass panels and set the candle within it. A primitive darkroom lantern at his disposal, yet I felt that had it not been there he would have been enterprising enough to extemporize. First he made a bath of developer in the stained sink. (There was just enough left to mix with water from the tap.) He took the glass plate out of its holder and immersed it in the murky liquid. It was quite a long time before anything appeared on it, owing to the low temperature of the developing bath, but at last it started to be clear that Holmes was dealing with a plate which had been exposed. Although I could not see much of the image from where I stood, I studied Holmes's expression as he gently rocked the glass plate to and fro. In the shimmering red light he looked for all the world like the demon king in a pantomime, especially when his eyebrows rose and his eyes protruded in surprise.

We heard him mutter, 'Upon my word!' We had previously seen him prepare a basin of hypo-fixative and now he washed the developer from the sink and poured the fixative over the plate, having rinsed the glass with water from the tap. Now he invited us to look at the image that he had produced. In turn, for the hide was somewhat claustrophobic, we peered at the sheet of glass as Holmes paddled his fingers to stir the fixing liquid.

He said, 'This may all have looked primitive to you, gentlemen, but I assure you I have even fixed a plate with common salt before now.'

When given the chance, I gazed at the image captured on the glass. I realized what had caused his surprise. The negative picture was not a Sussex landscape or illustration of some rural pursuit. Instead it was a portrait of a buxom young woman dressed only in muslin folds! I hasten to assure the reader that there was nothing distasteful about the portrait, for there was more than enough of the muslin involved, but . . . may I say perhaps that it was ever so slightly risqué, viewed in contrast with the rural scenes.

Then, finally, Holmes removed the candle from the red lantern and after washing the plate in water from the tap he held it up to the light that we might see it more clearly.

He said, 'It is very clear considering my ill-treatment of it. Back at Baker Street I could have developed and fixed it more expertly.'

Arthur Fox's eyes were like slits as he viewed the negative. 'Why, it is Jane Grundy, the under-parlourmaid, though not of course in her accepted attire. I never realized how comely she was before!'

Holmes asked, 'What more do you see? For example, where was it taken? Come, you are in a better position than I to recognize the setting. Notice particularly those heavily draped octagonal windows.'

Fox replied, 'Why, it is the interior of the old summer-house. Those windows are unique. There is also the book-case and a plant pot.'

I looked carefully at the picture and noticed that the young lady had particularly long hair which she no doubt needed to braid and rearrange to follow her daily calling. But here in the picture her hair aided the muslin in con-cealing her more obvious charms.

But I just said, 'Nothing of moment, Holmes.'

He grunted, repeating my words, 'Nothing of moment. Well, we shall see!'

Harding had nothing to add to what had been said regarding the picture, but spoke on the subject in general. 'A highly respectable English country gentleman has a photographic hobby which in addition to pastoral scenes includes portraits of comely and scantily clad young women. He hides away his darkroom that he might de-velop his portraits in complete privacy, yet he takes the pictures in a rather more conspicuous place. I have ob-served that summer-house myself without needing to seek for it.'

Lestrade said, 'No doubt it was well secured from within and its windows heavily draped. How, then, did he obtain the light required to take such a portrait. Could it be done with oil light, or did he perhaps resort to that flash stuff that you tampered with, Mr Holmes?'

Holmes shook his head. 'There are soft tones in the portrait which flashlight could not have produced, and its clarity of focus could not have been gained with a long exposure which oil light would have required. It has a glass roof, perhaps, my dear Fox?'

Arthur Fox nodded. 'Yes, the structure is perfect for use as a studio. Why, with the door secured from the inside and the windows draped one would require a ladder to see inside. Only one thing bothers me. There are no other plates of this kind here, and there is nowhere in the summer-house where they could be concealed. I have seen it from the inside and there is not so much as a cupboard. There is just that bookcase that you can see on the plate. Surely he would not go to such trouble and then destroy the fruits of his labour?'

Holmes shook his head. 'That had occurred to me also, and I think the time has come for us to visit the old summer-house. Perhaps it will tell us more than its image formed from gelatine on glass!'

We made our way through the undergrowth, a task more difficult than ever because we did not even have the occasional gleam of the police lamp. However, we managed it despite many a torn hand and calf.

As we walked, so slowly and carefully, striking a vesta now and then, Holmes demanded of Lestrade, 'Inspector, you have been remarkably reticent during the past hour. Do you not have something of importance to share with us?'

Lestrade grunted and said, 'Only that I do not speak until I am sure that I am going to utter words of wisdom. I believe I mentioned earlier that being a detective-inspector for many years makes a man unshockable, surprised at nothing. We may be about to unearth an Aladdin's cave of unspeakable bestiality in that there summer-house!'

I felt that Holmes, at this point, quite disgraced himself with a rare outburst of merriment. 'Oh my word, Lestrade, you have such a sense of the dramatic. If bestiality is what you are expecting to find you could well be disappointed! Ha, ha!'

At last we were out of the thicket and on to the lawn at the back of the house and came first upon the new summer-house, but within a minute Fox had led us up to the more secluded old one.

Holmes enquired of Fox, 'Were both of these buildings searched at the time of Reynaud's death?'

He replied, 'Thoroughly and, incidentally, with no sign that the old building had been used as a studio.'

We had no keys of course and Holmes did not deem it wise to return to the house and request one at this point. 'We may uncover something embarrassing to the memory of the late master of the house. Such is not my particular incentive. Come, I can open this lock with my penknife.'

I did not doubt for one moment that he could do this, having seen him do as much with many a sophisticated closure. As Holmes tampered with this simple lock Lestrade glanced heavenwards and whistled softly, rather as if he was entirely unconnected with any of us.

He muttered, 'I s'pose you know you are breaking the law?'

Then there was a snap and a click, the door was pushed open and we stepped inside. Fox was able to find the oil lamp, even in the dark, and soon had it lit. By its steady illumination we were able to see the summer-house interior clearly. We observed the simple furnishings which we had seen depicted on the photographic plate and had to agree with Fox that there was no visible sign of the use of the apartment as a photographic studio.

That was until Holmes's sharp eyes rested on a thin sheet of white painted wood and his even sharper mind gave us its purpose. 'The wood sheet has been painted white to serve as a portable light reflector. It can be moved about to reflect the natural daylight to gain artistic effects.'

He illustrated his words by moving the sheet around and reflecting the light of the oil lamp, then he leant it against the wall where he had found it.

He continued, 'His cameras and other portable equipment he kept at the hide so there is nothing here at a glance to betray his activities. Can you see anything else, Inspector?'

Lestrade glanced around shrewdly and said, 'There is a bookcase but all of its shelves are filled by volumes and there is no space for anything else. Otherwise there is not so much as a cupboard.'

It was true, the apartment was sparsely furnished as befitted a summer-house.

Sherlock Holmes irritated all of us at this point by seating himself upon a stool, closing his eyes and saying, 'I will now await the daylight. You gentlemen may, if you please, return to the house and possibly avail yourselves of a few hours of sleep.'

Lestrade at once agreed that this was an excellent suggestion and departed in the direction of Shaw Manor. The rest of us hesitated but Holmes sped our departure by making it clear that he would really prefer to be alone.

He lit a cigarette and said to me, 'Watson, when you return at daybreak you might bring my tobacco and a clay.'

CHAPTER FOUR

I arrived back at Shaw Manor to find, not surprisingly, a rather subdued atmosphere. Of course none of Gerald MacMillan's oddly invited guests had known the late Mirelda Reynaud, but they were all of them persons of the kind who would be deeply affected by such a tragedy so near to their place of temporary residence. Added to this they had of course experienced with astonishment the events leading up to MacMillan removing Holmes as a hostage and the return of Sergeant Fairbrother and his constable with their prisoners. The policemen had removed MacMillan and the valet to Lewes Prison by the time I re-entered the house. The staff were obviously at a complete loss, as underlings usually are at such a time of turmoil. They had not liked MacMillan but had obeyed and carried out his orders without which they appeared quite lost.

I felt that it was my duty to take on some sort of mantle of control if only that it might have a calming influence. I first ordered coffee to be made for guests and staff alike and when it was made I ushered everyone into the living-room. I took up my position on the little platform from which the rogue MacMillan had been wont to make addresses and I made something of a speech.

I began, 'Ladies, gentlemen and staff of Shaw Manor, the removal from the scene of your host, your employer, on top of the terrible news of the unlawful killing of Mirelda

Reynaud, behoves me to say a few words which might clarify the situation for you all. Of course I cannot, as yet, define the situation exactly but I would, if asked to make a calculated guess, say that we have all seen the last of the man you knew as Gerald MacMillan!' There were gasps of relief from the staff members and much puzzled tutting from the guests. 'I have no doubt that Mr Sherlock Holmes who has, I am happy to say, been rescued from his predicament, will have much more to tell you in the morning. Or rather, later *this* morning. Meanwhile, I feel sure that the Reynaud estate will have practical plans to assist all staff members and that we as guests may remain here for at least another day. Now I think that you should all try to gain a few hours of sleep, and I suggest that breakfast be served at an hour appropriate to the events that have occurred.'

The staff gratefully dispersed to their quarters, the butler ushering them away. The guests, including Harding and Lestrade, also departed to catch a little sleep. But it had been a more than trying time for them, and they were not blessed with the constitution which being a soldier of the Queen had given me. Fox departed for his abode, having livestock to tend and other essential chores to perform, so I was left alone to demolish gratefully most of a pot of coffee.

The hour was very late, or very early as you please to view it, and even I felt tired. Whilst all but drowsing I noticed that I was not quite alone, for one of the maids was just preparing to depart for her quarters. Her face, aye and her form, seemed to me to be rather familiar.

I called to her. 'Jane. It is Jane, is it not?'

She turned to face me, bobbed her head and said, 'Why yes, sir, if it please you. Is there something I can get you?'

I shook my head. 'No, but pray do come here and be seated. I would like to talk with you.'

She obeyed and I motioned to her to be seated which she did, very neatly and primly, drawing my attention to the fact that she had remarkable deportment for a servant girl.

I calmed the look of slight anxiety on her face by saying, 'Come Jane, you have nothing to fear. I will not eat you, what?'

She laughed politely and I continued, 'I have just recently been looking at a photographic image of yourself which we discovered in the hidden darkroom used by the late Mr Reynaud.'

She was alarmed, rather as if her worst fears had suddenly been realized.

She said, 'Oh sir, I thought that all of that had been forgotten, them never having found any of the pictures when they was a-lookin' for that will!'

I said, 'Ah, so there were other pictures?'

She answered, 'I don't know which one you have seen sir, but I must admit that there were six or seven of them in all. Mr Reynaud being such a fine man and such a perfect gent there didn't seem to be anything wrong with it at the time, but after his death the pictures could have been misunderstood. That was why I was hopin' none of them would be found. I never minded posing for him, but I was always a little worried about what the mistress might make of them.'

I said, 'Well, at least you don't have to worry in that direction now,' but could have bitten my tongue off for saying it.

She began to weep and I placed an arm around her. In so doing with every possible delicacy I could not help but realize what a very attractive young woman she was.

I said, 'There, there, dear girl, do not distress yourself. Only the one photograph has been discovered and that well within the bounds of good taste.'

She said, 'Ooh sir, they all was. I would not 'ave had

anything to do with nothing smutty. I think it's a shame that such a nice old gentleman should have had to keep his hobby so quiet. He was good to me and used to give me a few bob now and then aside from me wages, which was a great help to my parents who are very poor.'

I asked, 'You have no idea, I suppose, where he stored his other plates of you?'

She said, 'No. He just said though that one day they would make me famous, but I said that if he did not mind I would prefer not to be all that famous for the time being!'

I sent the poor girl off to bed and then retired to my room, though not to sleep for I was now quite awake. So I washed, shaved and changed from my evening clothes into a tweed suit. Then, it being six of the clock, I collected together a few of the comforts that Holmes would need: a pipe, tobacco, a cheese sandwich and a flask of coffee. As I boiled the water in the kitchen for the latter I fingered my sore chin ruefully and mused that I could have saved myself cold-water shaving. Alas, the English gentleman is helpless without servants. In the army I had relied on a batman and at Baker Street Mrs Hudson and Billy had made my life easier. Since my marriage I had been able to rely on my wife to make all the domestic arrangements. Now, having sent all the servants to bed, I had only myself to blame for my bad organization.

At a few minutes after six I entered the old summer-house with my offerings. Holmes appeared not to have moved from the stool since I had left him thus seated more than an hour earlier. But moved he had, which I knew from the disturbance of the cigarette ash which he had deposited liberally upon the floor.

He greeted me in crab-like manner. 'Ah Watson, you have brought my tobacco, that is good. You know, since I saw you I have been showing not a little interest in the bookcase. Even by oil light there seemed a decided difference in the appearance of the books on the top and bottom shelves. Look for yourself, Watson. What do you see?'

I looked and saw just two serried ranks of books without gaps or seeming differences and I said as much.

Holmes said, 'Look again, more carefully, and you will notice that the top shelf has its books very neatly placed. Move one and you will find that it would be difficult for them to be in a more orderly arrangement.'

I did as he had bade me and had to agree.

He said, 'Now observe the books on the lower shelf. They are also neatly arranged, in fact even more neatly than those above them. What do you make of that?'

I replied, 'Why, I take it to mean that all of his books were neatly arranged but those on the top shelf came in for more use than the others, which might perhaps seldom be disturbed at all.'

He chuckled. 'Hardly surprising, Watson, as you will find if you attempt to remove one of the books from the lower shelf.'

I tried, as he had suggested, to remove one of the lower books but found to my surprise that I was quite unable to do so. My friend was amused at my efforts to remove one of the row of exactly matching volumes.

He said, 'It is hardly surprising that you cannot remove *David Copperfield* because the book spines are a fake, albeit a clever one.'

He jumped to his feet and joined me at the front of the bookcase. He touched a portion of the moulding and to my surprise the book spines fell, as would a door, which in fact is exactly what the spines had been hiding.

I said, 'Very clever, Holmes. The particular disguise is

not unknown to me but you must admit that it is extremely well made.'

He said, 'A little too well made, for if even one of the spines had been made to appear as if it had been disturbed and replaced I could have overlooked it altogether.'

As the door dropped, a simple cupboard was revealed, a little deeper than the bookshelf it mimicked. Within it we could see a rack which held a series of glass full plates and a number of photograph albums.

Holmes pointed to the former and said, 'Negative!'

Then he pointed to the latter and said, 'Positive!'

He then explained, 'The plates are seven in number, all are of the housemaid in various artistic poses, similar in style to the one we have already seen. But if you remove one of the albums you will see that it contains a number of mounted sepia prints, but these are of other models. In all, the albums seem to go back over quite a long period of time, which I deduce from their gradually altering style is suggestive of other decades. Also the particular sensitized photographic paper onto which the images have been transferred is in some cases of a now obsolete type.'

Although inured to Holmes's deductions and their invariable truth I could not help but ask, perhaps just to give him practice, 'Could he not have purchased the paper and kept it for a long time?'

He closed the secret cupboard and seated himself once more upon the stool. He filled the pipe which I had fetched him and gratefully lit it.

Then through a haze of strong blue smoke he said, 'Watson, you know very well that I never hazard guesses, which is what you have implied. If sensitized photographic materials are stored for more than a few months, no matter how carefully, a certain discoloration transpires in the eventual print.'

Hastily I changed the subject. 'Do you intend to show the albums and negatives to the police?'

He said, 'I see no reason why I should, Watson, for however harmless these portraits may seem to men of the world like ourselves their revelation might cast a cloud on the reputation of the late Mr Reynaud, and I can see no purpose being served.'

I said, 'Lestrade saw the glass plate that you developed earlier.'

He said, 'It is not Lestrade's case, and anyway I doubt if he will mention the matter.'

He broke off to apply another lit vesta to his pipe, then continued, 'Especially if I ask him not to. I doubt if the local police will even find the secret cupboard.'

I asked, 'Shall you tell Harding and Fox about it?'

Holmes said, 'In my own time, after appealing to them for secrecy. I know, Watson, that you regard me as a cold fish at times, but I have some sort of compassion. The servant-girl would find it hard to gain a new position if it were known that she had posed, lightly clad. The girls in the other pictures may in some cases be servants also.'

I quickly caught the meaning of his words, 'In some cases?'

He said, 'Some of the portraits have captured the hands of their subjects as carefully as their faces. In these instances they are not the hands of serving girls. In other cases I noticed the hands to be hidden among draperies and these are probably of maids.'

I was deeply touched by his concern for others and was prompted to tell him of my conversation with Jane.

He nodded, rose to his feet and said, 'Then obviously, Watson, we are of one mind upon this matter.'

We returned to Shaw Manor, after carefully securing the door of the old summer-house. Holmes washed, shaved and changed into a Norfolk jacket and knickers, being the most casual and comfortable garments that he had brought from Baker Street. We sat in the living-room and saw the dawn light filter through the still-curtained windows. At least I did, for Holmes took a series of cat-naps. Between snoozes he would converse with me in an animated manner. He shared this strange ability with certain animals, this talent for being wide awake in an instant.

Eventually the butler, apologetic from habit despite my having suggested a late breakfast, entered, coughed politely and said, 'If you would care to move to the dining-room, gentlemen, you will find that we have restored normality to the domestic arrangements.'

We did as he suggested and found Lestrade and Harding at the table among the other guests. The latter were, for the most part, extremely subdued, the exception being Miss Finch who twittered as ever. However, her bird-like sounds were now more like a moorhen than a mavis! We all ate sparingly and slowly, and eventually Holmes rose to address us all.

'Ladies and gentlemen, I imagine that by now the police and my colleague Dr Watson have given you most of the known details of the tragic events of last evening. Enough then for me to confirm that Sergeant Fairbrother is now holding our host on a serious charge. I suggest that for the present you remain here in case the sergeant may return in order to ask further questions. Apart from this possibility I would like to address you all further in the living-room after luncheon, which I feel sure will be served at the usual hour.'

This was so, but appetites were still noticeably small, though quite a lot of wine was consumed. Afterwards Fox appeared and I unfortunately became embroiled in a conversation with the Glastonburys. I say 'unfortunately' because I wanted to speak with Fox myself concerning some recent developments. However, I was too late and promptly at about three of the clock Holmes took up his position to address us. I suddenly remembered that it was Boxing Day, though naturally the mood of us all was far from one of celebration. All the guests, Arthur Fox also, were seated, whilst the servants stood at the rear and on both sides.

Holmes spoke briskly and without formality. 'You are all, as dupes of Gerald MacMillan, guest or servant, entitled to a much fuller explanation of the events of the past days than I have before this been in a position to give you. This house, this fine country mansion, was the residence of the late Mr Reynaud and his lady wife Mirelda . . .'

Mr Glastonbury interrupted, 'Mr Speaker, a point of order. You mean his late wife Mirelda Reynaud!'

Rather to my surprise Holmes inclined his head but did not comment, but continued, 'Some years back Reynaud made a will, in favour of his nephew Gerald. However, more recently, having heard that his nephew and Gerald MacMillan were one and the same and of his exploits as a confidence trickster he made a second will, leaving everything instead to his other nephew Arthur Fox, despite an earlier estrangement. (Connected only with the use of the English version of the family name.) He had informed his wife of the change but unfortunately at the time of his recent death the second will did not yield itself to the most thorough search. Only the Reynaud's solicitor could explain to you the exact position regarding the two wills, but enough at this point for me to explain that a time limit was imposed concerning the finding of the second document and that this time limit is all but exhausted. After a few more weeks, MacMillan becomes the owner of Shaw Manor and heir to the Reynaud fortune.'

'If he has not gone to the gallows first!' It was Glastonbury again, but Holmes ignored him.

'Despite having such expectations, Gerald had, or has, debts both alarming and pressing. They could have landed him in prison well before he inherited. Witness the two so-called actors who were bailiffs hastily bribed; a brilliant touch from a practised confidence man. So, unable to wait any longer he devised a diabolical scheme to murder his own aunt in order to precipitate his inheritance. She had taken up residence in the gate-keeper's house, the Manor having too many memories for her. But being such a kindly woman she had kept on all the servants and had planned to keep them all until the day of the upheaval.

'So MacMillan hatched a wicked scheme, to kill his aunt whilst establishing an absolutely watertight alibi for himself. Having invited us all by the means already clear to you, he planned that we would all be present and he would be within sight and hearing of us at the very minute that the ghastly deed was established to have taken place. He sent me with a Christmas gift for Mirelda, drawing my attention to the time of my departure. He knew that his cousin, Arthur Fox, would call upon his aunt at about seven, and would discover the crime and even, hopefully, be accused of it. Certainly he was with us all from the time of my return.'

'And before that, Mr Holmes, we were with him the whole time you were away!' The interruption was from Miss Finch this time.

Holmes nodded to her politely and continued, 'Yes, yes, and in fact for hours thereafter, dancing attendance upon you all and even deceiving you into thinking that he was present even when he was being impersonated by his valet, aided by disguise and the phonograph, as I explained last evening before my unfortunate abduction! You have been informed of the dreadful details of the ghastly deed that MacMillan carried out.'

Harding, to my surprise, interrupted at this point. 'Mr Holmes, it was through my own suspicions that you were first brought onto the scene. I knew you had some inkling as to what might happen from quite an early stage. Could you tell us now, please, just how much of the puzzle you had solved at the time when we first heard of the tragedy?'

I was shocked at this outburst, for if my interpretation was correct he was accusing Holmes of allowing this murder to take place simply to finish a game that he was playing out. I knew that my friend was not capable of this.

But Holmes held his temper. 'Mr Harding, I admired your sense in calling upon me to participate in a strange puzzle. A participation with which I agreed because I was intrigued. I will answer your question as honestly as I can. At an early stage I had suspicions of a general nature leading me to think in terms of an impending tragedy. Then various indications began to form a pattern. The wills, concerning which I was not supposed to have knowledge, the bailiffs who nearly gave him away, and of course the gramophone. . . . When you were all in your beds I examined the instrument and discovered both the cylinder with MacMillan's voice recorded upon it and the two costumes. Suddenly it all began to fit together and I knew that Mirelda Reynaud was in deadly peril. I even saw that which turned out to be the murder weapon and wondered if it was just that, so carefully placed.'

Now Harding was furious rather than merely curious. He rose to his feet and shouted, 'All this you knew, and you all but expected this ghastly tragedy to occur just in the way that it did. But you did nothing to prevent it, and you call yourself a detective. What is the purpose of the mind of the great Sherlock Holmes if he is not able to act upon his brilliant deductions?'

I felt obliged to admonish Harding, saying, 'My dear sir, this outburst is unworthy of you. If you think that my friend and colleague is unmindful of the tragic circumstances of this affair you do him a serious injustice . . .' But I confess that at that point I trailed off in mid-speech because deep down in my heart I felt a little disappointed with Holmes myself. This despite admiring the brilliant deductions which had enabled him to solve the mystery. But friendship requires loyalty which I was determined to give my friend to the end. He may have kept me in the dark, and I mused on the possibility of a different outcome had he taken me into his confidence. Maybe in the past I had not shown enough initiative to gain his complete trust. Naturally all these thoughts occupied seconds rather than minutes whilst everyone was looking to Holmes to defend his conduct. They had not long to wait before he spoke.

There was a sound of a distracting nature from the entrance hall which we all ignored, although it seemed to bring an alert expression to Holmes's face.

Then he said, 'Thank you, Watson, but you hardly need to defend me as I am more than capable of my own defence. I hope that during the next few minutes you will all, especially you, Harding, alter your opinions of me.'

Harding interrupted again; he was still angry, but quieter now and more ironic in his tone. 'The only way you can do that, sir, is to resurrect that sweet old lady with whose life you gambled and lost. You caught a murderer where you could instead have prevented the crime.'

Holmes smiled, rather unfeelingly I thought, and his next words made me wonder if my friend had taken leave of his senses. He said, 'Resurrect dear Mrs Reynaud? Why, my dear Harding, that is exactly what I intend to do!'

'What . . . are you mad, sir?'

'What can you mean?'

'Do you feel unwell, Mr Holmes?'

These comments and questions bombarded the great detective, whom the company now began to believe to be quite mad. I realized of course that Holmes was not out of his mind but rather had some sort of card to play, but however high its value I could not for the life of me see how it could save his face now.

Holmes raised his voice and all but shouted, 'Mr Fox, will you please enter and bring your companion with you?' Dramatically, Arthur Fox entered, and on his arm was a dear, sweet little old lady. The gasp that their appearance elicited could have produced a small gale! Sherlock Holmes with that characteristic gallantry for the fair sex took Mrs Reynaud's arm and steered her to a chair on the platform. She seated herself and he stood beside her with the air of a conjurer who has just restored to life the lady thought to have been dematerialized.

His expression said, 'Here she is, large as life and twice as natural. Back from the vast ethereal depths!'

Once more it was Harding who was the first to speak. 'Mr Holmes, it does appear that I owe you an apology which I of course make unreservedly. But perhaps I might dare to suggest that I think you owe us all an explanation.'

Holmes smiled. 'Quite so, and you shall have it. I have already explained those events which led me to believe that the crime had been planned and their explanation indeed drew an oral chastisement which I in fact did not deserve. I not only deduced what had been planned but I laid plans of my own to prevent the crime from taking place. I conspired with friend Fox and with the lady herself to take a plan of action which contained a certain amount of risk, but that risk was of a calculated kind. This chance seemed worth taking, for if successful I knew that it could lead to our host being at once arrested on a charge of attempted murder. Oh yes, Harding, that was the charge made when the police took him. Mr Fox, at my instigation, made a life-like effigy of the lady, at least when viewed from the rear. The high-backed chair was placed with its back to the entrance which I expected MacMillan to use. Some articles of clothing and particularly of head gear were supported and arranged. There were even artfully stuffed gloves in his line of vision. A vegetable marrow was propped up and crowned with the lady's spare headgear including the cap which elderly ladies use to keep their hair tidy. From our host's point of entrance it appeared for all the world as if Mrs Reynaud sat, or possibly snoozed, in this high-backed chair, whereas in fact she was safely in an upstairs room. MacMillan wielded his iron bar with bestial cruelty and the subsequent collapse of the marrow within the headgear gave him an eerie feeling that his dreadful deed had been carried out. He retreated hastily, by the same way as he had entered, little knowing that he had been observed from a draped alcove by Arthur Fox. MacMillan did not dawdle because he needed to get back to Shaw Manor as soon as he could. Had the ruse been discovered, Fox was there to protect his aunt.'

Mention of the lady reminded us all that she must have shown great courage in co-operating with this daring plan.

As if prompted by a theatrical cue she took up the narrative. 'I would like to say a few words if I may, and the first must be those of thanks to Mr Sherlock Holmes for using his brilliant powers to not only discover my planned demise but also to arrange for my rogue of a nephew being apprehended. I knew that he was ruthless, but I did not think that he would try to kill me. I know that my very dear nephew, Arthur, will gladly help me to make the rest of your stay at Shaw Manor a pleasant one; for yes, I want you all to stay well into the new year.'

Everyone present was delighted to receive such a gracious invitation from such a grand old lady and there were grateful murmurs of acceptance.

Mrs Reynaud continued, 'Of course, Shaw Manor will only be mine for a few more months and I only wish that I was to lose it to my dear nephew, Arthur. Alas, that beastly rogue Gerald will soon be the owner, even if he is unable to enjoy it for some years to come.'

There were murmurs of sympathy and then Holmes spoke again. 'My dear Mrs Reynaud, had the second will been discovered your cup of happiness might well have been full, might it not?'

She agreed. 'Yes, but everything possible was done to find it. I fear we cannot go down that path again.'

With a flourish, Holmes withdrew a folded document from within his jacket, saying, 'Everything save the involvement of Sherlock Holmes; come, madam, I have found the second will.'

He handed it to Mrs Reynaud with a courtly gesture. She raised her lorgnette and scanned several of the closely filled pages so characteristic of such legal documents.

She gasped, 'Mr Holmes, is there no end to my indebtedness to you. Where on earth did you find it, where that we could possibly have missed?'

I too found his answer of great interest, for I was as unaware as anyone else concerning the discovery.

'I found it in a hidden cupboard behind a row of false book spines in the old summer-house. The cupboard contained some photographic plates and an album of prints. Between the leaves of the album I found the will.'

Mrs Reynaud placed the will on her lap and clapped her hands with delight.

She said, 'Of course, I had quite forgotten his secret hiding place. He used to take what he thought to be rather risqué pictures. He little knew that I was well aware of that aspect of his hobby. The pictures were quite harmless were they not, Mr Holmes?'

My friend bowed his head and said, 'They appeared to me to be delightful and well within the bounds of good taste.'

Having placed the precious will into the capable hands of Arthur Fox she rose and threw her arms around Holmes in grateful embrace. 'Mr Holmes, God bless you! What was it you said about my cup of happiness being full? Why, sir, it definitely runneth over!'

It was Arthur Fox's turn to speak and he was as near to tears of joy as a man can be, at least in public. 'Of course I cannot thank you enough, Mr Holmes, for have you not saved my beloved aunt and for an encore established my birthright? Dear Aunt Mirelda will, I know, accept my invitation to stay here in what will always to my mind be *her* home, for the rest of her life which I hope will be a long one.'

The tears were not far off now as he looked around him and asked, 'Where is Jane?'

Although I did not confide it to the reader until this point in my narrative I confess that I had for some time suspected that Arthur Fox and the maid, Jane, were attracted to each other. He was not greatly concerned when she could not at once be located but appeared a little anxious at the dinner-table when it appeared that no one had seen Jane for quite some time.

At length, the butler coughed apologetically as he handed him an envelope addressed to 'Mr Arthur Fox'. It was written with purple ink and the envelope was not of the quality that one might expect to use to communicate with the new owner of Shaw Manor.

He whispered to us, 'This was found in Jane's bedroom and all her belongings have been removed. Please excuse me whilst I read this note.'

He slit the flap with a table-knife, glanced at the note which he withdrew and then passed it to Holmes who studied it with interest. Holmes then pushed the note across to me and I swiftly scanned it . . .

Dear Arthur,

Now that the detective chap has found the pictures I cannot stay here any longer without Mr Reynaud being present to assure everyone that there wasn't no harm in them. I will try and find a job where they don't need a reference as I am hardly likely to get one here now. We could never be together as we are from different worlds.

I will not forget you.

Love,
Jane

I whispered some words which I fondly thought might be of comfort but which sounded strangely inadequate when uttered.

Holmes was more forthcoming and practical, 'My dear Fox, I had realized of course that there was an affinity between the lady and yourself. On the single occasion when you spoke of her to me, an expression of tenderness crossed your face. Please remember my dear chap, that the times are changing. It may not be too long before it is quite the accepted practice for a gentleman to marry a mere house-maid. What concerns me most is how the poor girl will manage in what is a very harsh world for a servant-girl without references. Your aunt would of course furnish her with these, but is unlikely to have an opportunity to help her. If I were to find her for you, what would you do?'

Fox brightened, 'Do? Why marry her of course if I could only convince her to be mine!'

Holmes nodded and said, 'Then, Watson, we must make haste to find the lady for our friend, must we not?'

I was of course delighted to answer in the affirmative. Arthur Fox who had already shed the gloom which reading the letter had produced, seemed to take on an all but optimistic air. 'If anyone can find her, sir, then you are he!'

Mirelda Reynaud expressed no wonder as to why we should be so concerned for the safety of one of her maids. She seemed to have known, despite never being informed, of her nephew's interest in Jane just as she had been aware of her husband's secret aspect to his hobby.

She was as helpful and earnest as she could be, saying 'Jane came to me a few years ago, when very young indeed, to become the main support of her elderly parents who lived in a tied cottage. But they have recently died, both unfortunately contracting a fever, and I know of no other living relatives.'

Then she showed us what a very shrewd lady she was by saying, 'Mr Holmes, why do you not make a search of her bedroom in the possibility of finding some kind of clue to her direction of departure? She must have left very stealthily for I have questioned the other servants and none of them saw her depart.'

The bedroom which Jane had occupied was not in a basement, as would have been usual in a town house, but in the considerable attic area of Shaw Manor. It was a small but pleasant enough apartment and sparsely furnished with the bare essentials; a bed, a chair, a bedside cupboard and a curtained alcove with a rail for hanging clothes.

The alcove yielded nothing whatever, but the bedside cupboard presented us with a few overlooked trifles: a pen, a nail-file and a small printed leaflet. Holmes ignored the pen and file but picked up and examined the leaflet. It was printed on one side only and he spread it onto the top of the bedside table so that we could see it:

'DE FOURE'S MODEL AGENCY'
Refined models provided for artists and photographers
74b (Suite 7), Charing Cross Road
London WC2.

There was a small design in the top right-hand corner depicting a camera lens and an artist's palette. It was about ten inches by eight and printed on buff paper.

After a couple of minutes Holmes took his lens from a pocket and taking up the leaflet he studied it more closely.

Eventually he passed it to me and said, 'What do you make of it, Watson?'

Other than those points which I have already explained to the reader I could only add, 'Could be a cover-up for something more sinister. There are a few rather rum firms operating in that area!'

Holmes chuckled. 'I think not, Watson, for if it were a disguise for the provider of ladies of easy virtue I imagine the pictorial addition would be a little more daring. At the very least a handsome woman's head and shoulders. No, it looks dull enough to be exactly what it claims to be, but there are a couple of things about it that are worthy of our attention. What do you make of the paper upon which it is printed, Watson?'

I held the leaflet up to the light and examined the watermark but could make little of it. I said, 'Doubtless having composed a monograph upon the subject of water-marks on paper and having the advantage of that lens you can tell me something that I have missed; does the mark have a special significance?'

He said, 'It may, Watson, it possibly may. The fact that it has a watermark at all is what intrigues me; leaflets of this kind as distinct from business cards and brochures are usually printed in large numbers for mass distribution. The paper upon which such a leaflet would be impressed would normally be of the kind which is made from the pulping of already used publications. It would bear the telltale flecks of all but imperceptible marks so characteristic of such leaflets. This has been quite expensively printed, therefore we are considering a firm of some standing in their particular field.'

Fox had said little and indeed had displayed not a little air of impatience during our conversation concerning the leaflet. Now he asked, 'Do you believe that Jane will contact this firm in order to try and obtain work as a model?'

Holmes answered, 'No, but I believe that she has been in correspondence with them in the past. Had she intended to contact them upon leaving here I feel that she would have taken the leaflet with her.'

Fox asked, 'What makes you think, then, that she has written to them?'

Holmes indicated a tiny splash of ink on the corner of the leaflet which was small enough for me to have overlooked entirely.

Then Holmes took the pen from the cupboard and showed us the nib through his lens. 'You see, the colour is the same as the trace of ink on the leaflet, which probably got there when she wrote to this company. The nail-file is in a rather unusual place is it not? I suspect that she used it on her nails after writing the letter, being conscious of the fact that her servant's hands would preclude her from many of the opportunities that exist for a model. The late Mr Reynaud, on photographing her, realized that her hands were not her best feature and hid them among folds of muslin.'

Fox grunted. 'You think, then, that she has delusions of becoming a professional model?'

Holmes snapped back at him, 'Why delusions, for is she not an extremely attractive girl? Come, sir, it appears to me that your interest in Jane involves protecting her from all men, except for yourself!'

Fox, suitably chastened, said, 'Yes, I'm sorry, but I love her and would not want her to come to any harm.'

Holmes said, in contrasting tone to that which he had just used, 'Come, sir, I doubt that harm will come to such an intelligent girl who has been raised by god-fearing parents. Watson and I will leave for London this very night to commence our search for her. Rest assured that you are in good hands.'

Arthur Fox took us to Henfield Station in his old horse-drawn vehicle, and as we scrambled into a first-class smoker he gave us his goodbyes that were full of heartfelt thanks. He said, just as the whistle blew, 'Were it not for you gentlemen I would have lost my aunt and my birthright. Now I have both, and it is perhaps too much to ask that you can find my lost love for me as well.'

We had only time to call words of comfort which seemed to lose themselves in the yellow engine smoke as soon as we uttered them. That same acrid vapour made the lone figure of Arthur Fox, standing alone on the platform, seem like some forlorn ghost.

Needless to say, on the journey — between consuming some items from the picnic basket which the kindly Mrs Reynaud had thrust upon us — we discussed in great detail the happenings of the few days that had passed since Harding had burst in upon us with his problem. As for Harding himself, following a shame-faced apology concerning his lack of trust in Holmes he had decided to stay on at Shaw Manor until the last trace of festivity was ended.

Holmes said, 'He deserves to enjoy the rest of his holiday, Watson, for whilst everyone has lauded me to the skies it is Harding they really have to thank for the happy outcome. If he had not had the good sense to consult me, you know what would have happened.'

But of course one small shadow still threw its image onto an otherwise happy outcome; I refer to the missing housemaid, Jane.

'Shall you assist me in trying to find her?' Holmes asked.

I replied, 'I think not, Holmes, for I have played truant almost as long as I dare, and must soon return to prepare for Mary's homecoming and of course to take up my work again.'

He said, 'But you have a day or two before the old year is done, have you not?'

I nodded, and realized that he expected me to stay at Baker Street until at least New Year's Day.

Whilst unwarned, Mrs Hudson was equal to our return, with the gas lights in the hall at Baker Street fairly hissing as she turned up their brilliance. 'Mr Holmes, Doctor. I must have known you were coming home earlier than I expected when I made that huge steak pie this morning. Just give me five minutes and there will be hot water in your rooms.'

Within half an hour I felt as if I had never left the rooms, even to marry Mary, for so timeless was the atmosphere. It was just like coming home.

As we consumed the wonderful meal which the good lady placed before us I mused on how much happier I felt and more comfortable with the domestic arrangements at

221b Baker Street than I had been with those at Shaw Manor, where the huge rooms and regiment of servants had given me a feeling as if staying at some grand hotel rather than in someone's home.

After dinner we smoked our pipes and I tried to lead Holmes to discuss the missing housemaid and how we might start to search for her. But he would have none of it, ever changing the conversation when I raised the subject. But later he made up for it by playing several of my favourite pieces on his violin.

When at last Holmes would deign to talk about the affair that was much upon my mind, I dared to say, 'You know, Holmes, it would be very helpful if we had a photograph of Jane, would it not?'

He smiled indulgently. 'Whilst you were packing your traps at Shaw Manor I was not exactly idle. I gained the permission of the Reynauds to bring with me one of the glass plate photographs of the lady in question. There were no positive prints available to me save those in the album, of which I declined to deprive the dear lady. When the daylight returns I will make a print, for I have a frame which will serve.'

The following morning Holmes was as good as his word, setting about the task of producing a print on daylight printing paper, a supply of which he fortunately had. After an hour in the frame the paper was fixed in a dish of hypo and we examined it carefully. I had already seen the lady on the glass plates but the print was of course a positive and therefore even easier to recognize.

As Holmes agitated the print in the liquid, he pointed at a portion of it with the tweezers. 'Look at her arm, Watson. Yet another reason why she may not obtain the employment she desires.'

It was true. On her arm there was a quite distinctive all but diamond-shaped birthmark.

I said, 'I suppose this means that you will start at the bottom of the ladder, searching for art students who want an inexpensive model?'

He said, 'Bravo, Watson. And such people will be likely to remember a model with a diamond-shaped birthmark upon her forearm.'

Holmes used another hour or two in making a second print which he allowed to hang and dry alongside the first. When they were both ready we of course had a photograph each to show if we became separated during our quest.

We started off by visiting De Foure's Model Agency in Charing Cross Road.

Mr De Foure himself proved to be in charge of this concern and indeed he seemed to be the only member of the organization. Holmes was later to refer to him as the one-man band. He was an elderly, sparse-haired, thin-faced individual of almost clerical appearance and attire. His office was sparingly furnished with a shelf of ledgers and files, plus a roll-topped desk which appeared to be filled to the point where it would be impossible to close it.

He looked at the picture of Jane and then said, 'Why yes, I did have some correspondence with Miss Marlene Schultz; a continental lady I imagine from her name and style of writ-ing English. It is quite some time since I heard from her and I was unfortunately never able to obtain any work for her.'

Holmes asked, 'Do you have any of her letters by any chance?'

He shook his head mournfully, saying, 'No, I did not file them, and I contacted her through a post-office box at some village in Sussex, I seem to remember.'

I asked, 'Henfield?'

He brightened. 'Why, yes, I believe it was! Gentlemen, if you do manage to trace this young lady I hope you will remember my agency commission!'

We discovered that there were a number of other agencies of the same type within the confines of Charing Cross Road; one of my favourite thoroughfares, ever since in my student days when I used to haunt its secondhand bookshops. An interesting place, with the accommodation above the shops being of a most unusual nature with the trade notices and styles of agents, consultants and bespoke workers of many trades.

Holmes and I split up and did not meet again until it was time for dinner at 221b Baker Street. Over a tasty roast we compared notes, but discovered that we had both drawn a blank.

Holmes somewhat surprised me by saying, 'I see little to be gained by your continuing to busy yourself with this matter, Watson. I know you have other interests to pursue and I have taken enough of your time already. I can see that I am going to have to devote quite a lot of time to investigating the more unsavoury fringe of the artistic world. What, I ask you, does a girl like Jane do if she is unable to get work from legitimate agencies?'

I replied, 'Why I imagine she would return to being a housemaid?'

He shook his head. 'She has no references.'

I said, 'Then this may be the answer to our problem, for she may contact Shaw Manor again.'

He said, 'If she knew of the new developments there, then that is possible, but as she does not . . .'

I interrupted, 'She knows at least that MacMillan has been arrested.'

He agreed. 'Yes, but nothing concerning the miracle of

Mrs Reynaud's return from the dead, or for that matter that the will has been discovered. No, Watson. I fear for her safety in a city that has so much temptation for a young woman in her situation. I intend to investigate among the less respectable artists and even . . .'

I interrupted with spirit, 'Holmes, you don't mean that she might . . .'

He said, 'Not from choice, I feel sure. But cold and hunger can play havoc with ethical considerations.'

I knew that he was right in that there was little I could do to help, for I knew that Holmes operated best alone in such circumstances. Moreover, I was guilty enough concerning my neglected responsibilities to take advantage of the fact that it was he who had suggested that I depart.

During the ensuing twelve months I saw less of Holmes than during any other year of our long association. In February I called on him but found him deeply involved in a case concerning the theft of some gold bullion, which seemed to have driven every other consideration from his mind.

I dropped by again in August only to be told by Mrs Hudson that he was off on one of his jaunts.

The leaves were falling when next I saw my friend, and he was again preoccupied, but with several different cases. He was like Cinqui Valli, keeping half-a-dozen balls in the air at once!

He said, 'The housemaid, Watson? I am still alert in the matter but have other problems to consider. Indeed, upon one of them the whole future of our country may depend.'

It was the proximity of another Christmas which brought the whole matter back to my mind, especially when an invitation to spend yule-tide at Shaw Manor arrived in the post. I accepted, knowing that my wife was once more going to dwell with relatives for the festive season.

I confess I was a little surprised that there was no mention of Holmes upon the card, but assumed that his invitation would be an individual one.

I wrote to accept, and wired Holmes: 'SEASONS GREETINGS STOP SHALL YOU BE AT SHAW MANOR FOR YULETIDE STOP REGARDS WATSON.' The boy on the bicycle soon brought a reply. 'MY DEAR WATSON STOP BUSINESS AT SHAW MANOR CONCLUDED STOP OTHER FISH TO FRY STOP A MERRY CHRISTMAS STOP REGARDS HOLMES.'

My surprise at Holmes's cavalier treatment of the invitation which I felt sure he had received was cast to the back of my mind soon after my arrival at Shaw Manor.

My host and hostess, Arthur Fox and his Aunt Mirelda, made me so welcome and indeed overwhelmed me with kindness. Much to my amused pleasure I found all of Gerald MacMillan's oddly chosen guests of that previous dramatic yule-tide present.

Of course, at first there was a good deal of reminiscing but this gave way to the pure enjoyment of one of the best Christmas gatherings that I had ever experienced. I'm happy to tell the reader, however, that Santa Claus did not appear and the gramophone was notable for its absence!

It was on the very eve of Christmas itself when a big surprise occurred. We were all sitting around the fire at that point when the dinner had been demolished and we were forcing down a mince pie too delicious to be denied.

I heard a carriage arrive and the butler soon thereafter entered, coughed and extended a small silver tray in Fox's direction. Arthur took the two small scraps of pasteboard and studied them.

He spoke to us all. 'Well, it seems we are to have the

pleasure of Sherlock Holmes's company after all, also that of a Mlle Gloria De Marcelle, whoever she may be. But any friend of Holmes is a friend of mine!'

Then he turned to the butler and said, 'Please admit the lady and gentleman.'

I need hardly tell my reader that my friend Sherlock Holmes is not really a ladies' man. He has always to my knowledge and in my observation treated the female sex with the respect that it deserved, but has told me more than once that romance could never play any part in the life of a man of science, which is what he considers himself to be. Of course there was the episode of the divine Irene Adler, and I know that Holmes has never forgotten her. Yet it was with some surprise that I saw a handsome woman enter the room on Holmes's arm. She was wearing an expensive-looking fur coat and a large brimmed hat with a heavy veil.

Holmes was the first to break the astonished silence. 'My dear Mrs Reynaud, Mr Fox, Watson, ladies and gentlemen, please allow me to introduce my delightful companion, Mlle De Marcelle.'

Fox admonished his butler, asking, 'Why did you not take Mademoiselle's coat, or rather get a maid to do so?'

The butler gulped and muttered, 'I was advised not to by Mr Holmes, sir.'

Fox grunted and then said, 'Well whatever pleases you, Mademoiselle, but you will find the room pleasantly warm. However, please do be seated and I will fetch some refreshment for you.'

The lady, her features still much concealed by her veil, accepted a glass of cordial and a mince pie as she sat near the edge of the gathering. I assumed she sat there because the fire would have made her a shade too warm in the outdoor attire which she seemed so loath to part with.

Holmes signalled to me to join him in the hall. I could see that he was anxious to converse with me.

When we were out of all earshot he said, 'Watson, I searched for Jane for months, but for once in my life I was on the wrong track in looking in the streets and taverns where I should have been looking in higher places. Then, about a month ago I thought I would go to an exhibition of paintings to see if I could recognize any of the models. It was held at the Northumberland Hotel and I chanced whilst there to wish to wash my hands. I entered the men's cloakroom and was washing my hands when I happened to glance at the wrapper which I removed from the soap. It bore an advertising portrait, accompanied by the words 'Gloria De Marcelle uses Shear's Toilet Soap'.

I could not help but interrupt him at this point. 'Holmes, you are telling me that you looked up your companion through seeing her depicted upon a cake of soap? You do surprise me, I have never known you to become infatuated by a portrait before, save that of *The* woman!'

He growled at me in irritation. 'Come, Watson, take a look through the doorway, I fancy you will recognize Mlle De Marcelle!'

I did as he bade me to find that she had removed her hat and veil. Her golden hair had cascaded down and even without the veil it took me perhaps ten seconds before I recognized her.

'Holmes, it is Jane!'

He smiled. 'Exactly, Watson, and as you can see it is Arthur Fox's cup that runneth over this time. He implored me to find his housemaid, but instead I found him a famous celebrity. Jane proved to be so photogenic and has become so famous that any man would kill to marry her. But Arthur Fox would have killed for her even when she was just a skivvy!'